TRACKING
TRIPLE
SEVEN

Jamie Bastedo

TRACKING TRIPLE SEVEN

a novel

Red Deer PRESS

Published by
Red Deer Press
A Fitzhenry & Whiteside Company
1512, 1800–4 Street SW
Calgary Alberta Canada T2S 2S5
www.reddeerpress.com

Credits
Edited for the Press by Peter Carver
Cover and text design by Erin Woodward
Cover photos courtesy of iStock and Corbis
Printed and bound in Canada by Friesens for Red Deer Press

Acknowledgments
Financial support provided by the Canada Council. We acknowledge the financial support of the Government of Canada through the Book Publishing Industry Development Program (BPIDP) for our publishing activities.

The Canada Council | Le Conseil des Arts
for the Arts | du Canada
Since 1957 | depuis 1957

National Library of Canada Cataloguing in Publication Data
Bastedo, Jamie, 1955–
Tracking triple seven
ISBN 0-88995-238-8
1. Title.
PS8553.A82418T72 2001   jC813'.6   C2001-910208-9
PZ7.B375Tr 2001

TEACHER'S GUIDE

A companion teacher's guide, *Grizzlies of the Arctic Tundra,* has been prepared by the author as part of a national education project on the arctic grizzly. Suitable for elementary to high school students, this richly illustrated resource includes detailed natural history information on grizzly bears, user-friendly classroom activities plus a chapter-by-chapter novel study of *Tracking Triple Seven.* To order *Grizzlies of the Arctic Tundra,* contact:

Raven Rock Publishing
21 Burwash Drive
Yellowknife
Northwest Territories
XIA 2VI
Canada
Phone 867-873-8440
Fax 867-669-9017
E-mail ravenroc@internorth.com

ACKNOWLEDGMENTS

Unlike many northern tales, whether about fish or frostbite, this book is a work of pure fiction. I made the whole thing up and had a lot of fun doing it. The truth is, though, a good part of what you are about to read actually happens out there on the tundra. Some grizzly bears get a real kick out of tobogganing or will lure fish with their deadly claws. Some biologists do lose their pants while carrying bear cubs in their arms. Peregrine falcons sometimes attack helicopters. Caribou will kill wolves. I have seen, heard or read about most of what follows in these pages.

Many of the stories woven into this book came from the lips of bear experts who often work nose to nose with wild grizzlies. Their contribution to my work, both in information and inspiration, is immeasurable. Thank-you Vivian Banci, Ray Case, Dean Cluff, Rob Gau, John Lee, Andy McMullen, Robert Mulders and Ian Ross. For bringing the satellite technology down to earth for me, I thank Anne Gunn and Helmut Epp. Thanks also to the folks at Great Slave Helicopter in Yellowknife, who fed me enough information about helicopters to convince me, almost, that I could fly one.

Thank-you Peter Carver, who, through several drafts, helped me discover the book's deeper story. Thank-you John Lee and my wife, Brenda, for correcting technical and story problems in the first draft. And thank-you Dennis Johnson and Carolyn Dearden for transforming my humble manuscript into this handsome novel.

I thank my many financial sponsors, who gave me the freedom to research and write and dream about grizzlies without hearing the scratch of wolves at my door. A special thanks to my major sponsor, the Canada Millennium Partnership Program. Thanks also to World Wildlife Fund Canada, the Northwest Territories' Department of Resources, Wildlife & Economic Development, Nunavut's Department of Sustainable Development, Diavik Diamond Mines and BHP Diamonds. I must add that the opinions expressed in this novel are the product of my head and heart and do not necessarily reflect the official views of any particular sponsor, including the Government of Canada.

Finally I thank my wife and daughters for their constant and loving support even on those trying days when I may have seemed more like a bear than a writer.

To my daughters,
Jaya and Nimisha,
whose idea this was.

Message from the Honourable Herb Gray, Deputy Prime Minister and Minister responsible for the Government of Canada's millennium initiative

Congratulations to Jamie Bastedo on the publication of his novel, *Tracking Triple Seven.* This novel, as a companion to the Educator's Guide, *Grizzlies of the Arctic Tundra,* will spark the imagination of readers of all ages as they immerse themselves in the arctic world of barren-ground grizzlies.

Until recently, very little was known about this magnificent animal. This novel addresses this oversight by giving our young people an inside look at the experiences, behaviours and adventures of a female grizzly and her cubs. Readers will have a greater understanding of and appreciation for grizzlies and the vast northern regions of our country.

The Government of Canada proudly supported this publication with a financial contribution through the Canada Millennium Partnership Program. Educating both young people and adults will ensure that the natural habitat of grizzlies is well protected into this new millennium. This book inspires us in the spirit of our national millennium theme, "Sharing the Memory, Shaping the Dream."

Best Wishes,

The Hon. Herb Gray, M.P.
Deputy Prime Minister

2000
Canada

CONTENTS

Prologue　　　Balancing Bears　17

Winter
Chapter 1　　Something's Up　20
Chapter 2　　Mother Lode　29

Spring
Chapter 3　　Lift-Off　36
Chapter 4　　Rebirth　52
Chapter 5　　Bear Hunt　61
Chapter 6　　Claim-Staking　69

Early Summer
Chapter 7　　Free Fall　82
Chapter 8　　Fishing Hole　89
Chapter 9　　Crack-Up　102
Chapter 10　Lunch Break　112

Midsummer
Chapter 11　Caribou Column　124
Chapter 12　Stakeout　132

Chapter 13   Ghost Hunt   151
Chapter 14   Double Blind   157
Chapter 15   Blissed Out   165
Chapter 16   Roundup   171

Fall
Chapter 17   Guard Down   192
Chapter 18   In Camp   199
Chapter 19   Dead End   207
Chapter 20   Bear Huggers   220
Chapter 21   Victory Lake   235

When you bring two very intelligent species together—humans
   and grizzlies—what happens could have infinite possibilities.
—Ian Ross, Bear Biologist

It's best not to talk much about him. Don't tease him. Don't think
   or speak ill of him. The best thing is just try to ignore each
   other. The grizzly is a great good animal that we have to learn
   to live together with.
—Harry Simpson, Dene Elder

Bears are made of the same dust as we, and breathe the same
   winds and drink of the same waters. A bear's days are warmed
   by the same sun, his dwellings are overdomed by the same
   blue sky, and his life turns and ebbs with heart-pulsings like
   ours and was poured from the same fountain.
—John Muir, Naturalist

The strength of Bear medicine is the power of introspection. To
   become like Bear and enter the safety of the cave, we must
   attune ourselves to the energies of Mother Earth and receive
   nourishment. . . . Bear is then reborn like the opening of spring
   flowers.
—Jamie Sams and David Carson, Animal Medicine Teachers

BALANCING BEARS

The bear lives at both ends of the food chain, and dwells at both
ends of the universe—in the heavens and underground. It is the
bear that keeps the heavens turning, and the seasons changing.
—*Barry Sanders,* Bears in the Sky

Like the long barrel of a gun, the earth's axis points directly at a far-away star sitting more or less dead on the north pole of the sky. Five thousand times more luminous than our own small sun, it is not the brightest star that we can see with the naked eye—almost fifty are brighter. Nor is it the farthest star. At 680 light-years away, it would take you over one hundred billion years to reach this star in today's fastest spaceship. Yet, intergalactically speaking, this star is right in our backyard.

Setting this star apart from all of the rest is what it doesn't do: move. It's the only one that stands perfectly still all night. From our earthly stage, the entire universe revolves around this one star: Polaris, the North Star, *Nuutuittuq.*

Whirling counterclockwise around this cosmic hub, never setting, keeping the whole thing in motion, some say, are two bears with ridiculously long tails.

The North Star tips the tail of Ursa Minor, a small bear, probably a cub, still very much inseparable from its mother, Ursa Major, the Great Bear. The heart of the Great Bear is the Big Dipper's scoop—its handle, her tail. This dangles irresistibly in front of the little bear's nose and, so, round and round they go.

Just who is chasing whom is hard to say. That this game should go on night after night—forever—is something worth wishing for. Because, it is said, the perpetual play of these bears, spinning in proper alignment around the North Star, ensures the safe passage of all newborns, bears included, as they spiral down through the birth canal into the world.

WINTER

CHAPTER 1

SOMETHING'S UP

Technology can take the field out of field work.
—Ian Ross, *Bear Biologist*

January 30.

A great gush of solar wind slams into the earth's atmosphere and explodes into neon light. One hundred and twenty-five miles up, the Northern Lights throw pinwheels of ghostly greens and reds across a black arctic sky.

Higher still, five hundred miles above the earth, a sudden flash of reflected sunlight foretells the breaking of a new day. The speck of light grows brighter, steadier.

Here it comes. A satellite.

This is no flashy rocket ship. It looks more like a sculpture built in a junkyard. With this spacecraft, it's not streamlining that counts. It's not looks. It's brains. And this is one smart satellite.

Dangling off one side is a blue solar panel the size and shape of a Ping-Pong table. Off the other is a metal tower shaped like a dunce cap. Between them is a shiny box bristling with antennae, camera lenses, and radar dishes. Meet ECOS-3, the fanciest environmental satellite ever launched into space.

A jet of flame rushes from the satellite's propulsion vent. In the blink of an eye the flame vanishes, burning only long enough to make hairline tweaks in ECOS-3's flight path over the poles. Its finely tuned sensors gobble up the latest news about the state of the planet: the path of a fire galloping through the rainforest, the health of the atmosphere that hugs our earth and protects us all.

This morning, out of all the crazy electronic noise leaking from our planet, a delicate satellite sensor trained on northern Canada picks up a steady beep from the vast frozen tundra. This locator beacon comes from a leather satellite collar, number 7-7-7, worn by a grizzly bear tucked in her winter den. To the biologists who clamped it around her neck, she is known as Triple Seven.

The locator beacon has not budged for over three months—since the treeless barren-lands froze over in mid-October and Triple Seven moved into her den. But today the satellite records something quite peculiar. All the bear's life signs, normally steady for weeks, now show strange wobbles. Heart rate: up. Breathing rate: up. Body temperature: up. Muscle activity: up. Everything's in high gear.

The signals from Triple Seven's collar, wobbles and all, are silently processed by ECOS-3, then beamed down to earth at the speed of light. A satellite dish beside the ECOS relay station in Fairbanks, Alaska, scoops these signals out of thin air. Like pinball wizards, computer technicians sort through a fresh batch of satellite data, then open an electronic floodgate that sends it south. The data ricochets through more relay stations, then hurtles north to Yellowknife, Northwest Territories. Its final destination: the Great Bear Research Center housed in a tall office building that pokes above the frozen spruce forest.

Round trip from sleeping grizzly to satellite, satellite to relay stations, relay stations to Yellowknife: 12.4 minutes. The morning's bear data is in the bag.

In the bag, but not out of it.

Glitches happen. About the time the data arrives, a raven flies into the town's main power line and explodes in a fireball of electric current.

Eighteen hundred miles away, fourteen-year-old Benji Gloss wakes to the *whup-whup-whup* of a helicopter flying over his house. He opens one eye and looks at his watch. Right on time, he thinks. The 7:15 Rat Race Patrol. He concentrates on the helicopter noise until it is swallowed by a rising storm of traffic.

Benji opens both eyes and sees rain pelting his small attic window. Of all the rooms in the Gloss mansion, he chose this as his bedroom. That was after his mother died. Since her death last year, he has found a strange security here that he can't explain.

"Agoraphobia. That's what *you've* got," said his friend, Brad, when he first saw Benji's dinky room. They have this game of trying to out-weird each other with strange words.

"I give," said Benji. "What's that?"

"A fear of open spaces."

"Phobia schmobia," Benji told Brad. "I like my mountain cave. Gives me a pilot's eye view."

Benji watches the rain on his window for a while, then reaches for his TV remote control. He holds it to his mouth like a microphone and starts beating his chest to sound like he's broadcasting from a helicopter.

"Go-od-mor-ning-San-Fran-cisco! This is your eye-in-the-sky, Benji Gloss, floating above the highways and byways of our Golden City. It's another drizzly Friday morning on the Sunshine Coast. Time for your rush-hour traffic report from radio WGDB—*We Get Down and Boogie!* Well, nobody's boogying down there this morning, folks. From up here all I see are long, skinny parking lots. Somebody jack-knifed an ice cream truck on the Golden Gate Bridge, and traffic's backed up all the way to Oregon. Forget about the Oakland Bay Bridge. That sank outta sight last night due to a minor earthquake...."

The voice of Benji's father breaks in over an intercom above his bed. "Who you talking to up there, Benji?"

Benji spins the remote control above his head, like a helicopter rotor. "Oh . . . just bats, Dad."

"I'm off to a breakfast meeting, son. The housekeeper's made some Belgian waffles for you."

His father has tons of money from all the mines he owns. But he never seems to have any time.

"But I thought you said we'd both play hooky today and check out that new aerospace museum."

"Change of plans, Benji. . . ."

"Lemme guess. Another mine tour?"

Over the intercom, Benji hears the trill of his father's cell phone. "Hang on, son."

Any bets, thinks Benji, still spinning the remote control. Another hole in the ground.

"Good guess," says his father after a long pause. "Have I ever taken you to the Diehard Copper Mine in Arizona?"

"Twice, Dad."

"Oh . . . well . . . how about we take my personal jet this time?"

Benji sits up and speaks right at the intercom. "You mean the Skyrider-6?"

"That's it. We'll buzz the Grand Canyon on the way."

"With me at the controls?"

"I'll talk to the pilot."

"It's a deal, Dad."

"I'll send my limousine to pick you up at nine sharp."

Back in Yellowknife, it's −45°f and still pitch black outside. Like schooling minnows, workers stream into the office building. Most wear puffy red parkas and heavy white boots, which they kick against the glass doors to get the snow off. Lights go on, filling each floor with a garish green glow. The hushed halls of a hundred offices gradually erupt with the sound of whirring computers. The smell of fresh coffee and stale doughnuts fills the air.

From one particularly large parka emerges Ozzie, a bear biologist. While peeling off his parka, he juggles a coffee cup the size of a soup bowl. With a barrel chest and a six-foot frame, Ozzie's a big man—and hairy enough to be mistaken for one of the animals he studies. Cinnamon-colored fuzz leaks from between the overstressed buttons and cuffs of his plaid shirt. He wears a faded ball cap with a crest showing a tiger with mighty fangs perched on top of a huge diamond. Stitched above the tiger are the words *Saber Mine.*

Ozzie flicks on his computer and drops into a shabby leather chair with a contented grunt. He takes a cautious sip of his steaming coffee and crinkles his nose. He growls under his breath, then reaches into the desk and pulls out a bag of Jumbo-Puff marshmallows. He rips the bag open with his teeth and pours five marsh-mallows into his coffee.

This is no ordinary coffee cup. It has a textured, almost hairy look to it with two big brown arms that hug the cup and end in orange claws. Between the claws, in blood-red letters, it says, "BEAR HUGGER."

He lets the marshmallows steep for a moment, then sniffs. "Hmmmm." Another cautious sip. His eyes close. "Ahhhhh," he says loudly enough to be heard way down the hall and possibly even one floor below.

Fueled by high-proof coffee and marshmallow mush, Ozzie turns to the task at hand: downloading the morning's grizzly bear data. His carrot-sized fingers fly into action, hammering out commands on the keyboard. He looks up at a screen that's blank except for a small hourglass filling with electronic sand.

He hammers in more commands. Nothing. He folds his hands and puts them in his lap, but his fingers keep flapping. Then he cracks them loudly one by one. "Where's the data?" he mutters. He twirls a finger in his great Viking beard, then whacks the side of the comput-er with the back of his hand. The hard drive whines. The screen fizzes. The hourglass fills. No data.

Ozzie reaches for his bear cup while staring at the screen and takes a deep swig. "Aagh!" he yells after scalding his tongue and most of his throat. No one comes running. The other biologists are used to such outbursts from Ozzie's office.

He boots his desk and spins around to face the window. From his top-floor perch, he sees a veil of ice fog draped over the town. All he can see of the streets below is an eerie orange cloud around each streetlight.

Above the ice fog, the night's last dance of Northern Lights fades in the west. Above them, a bright half-moon. Above that, stars. He can just make out the Great Bear glimmering through the creeping dawn.

Ozzie's view of the stars suddenly improves. The orange glare of city lights is snuffed out by another midwinter power failure. He slams a fist against the window. "Blasted ravens!"

Near the wilderness fringe of town, a raven on its breakfast tour to the dump crashes into some hydro wires veiled by ice fog. The instant the bird's wing tips bridge two wires, a hundred thousand volts of raw electricity scream through its body and exit its feet, which both blow clean off. Little puffs of flame shoot out of its hollow leg stumps as the raven drops like a black stone into the snow.

For five seconds there is only silence, darkness. Then emergency lights go on, flooding the hallways with cold light. A metallic female voice blares out commands above Ozzie's head. "Evacuate the building by your nearest exit. Stay calm. Do not run." He's still looking out the window and, except for plugging his ears, doesn't budge. "Evacuate the building by your nearest exit. Stay calm. Do not run. Evacu . . ." The normal lights go back on. Computers reboot. The coffee perks.

"You have new mail," announces another voice, this time from his computer. A swift kick against the wall and Ozzie is soon hammering keys and opening files. The final floodgate swings wide. At last the grizzly data pours on to his screen. He unlocks a safe beside his desk and pulls out a dog-eared field book marked, "Satellite Bear Data: Hands Off!"

He sticks a pencil in his beard and scrolls through the first screen of numbers. His finger slides down the screen creating a crackling trail of static electricity. He starts scribbling. "Grizzly 661. Accuracy index: 3." He makes an approving rumble in his throat. "Strong signals this morning."

Ozzie steals another look outside, pressing his big nose against the window. In a shrinking pocket of darkness, a pinprick of slowly moving light catches his well-trained eye. He presses closer, bending most of his nose to one side. There it is, ECOS-3, sailing past the North Star. Ozzie's hot, heavy breaths quickly steam up the window. By the time he wipes it clean, the speck of light is gone.

He swivels back to work. *Scroll, scribble. Scroll, scribble.* For the fifty bears he's collared, he knows most of the numbers by heart. All is routine. Boring in fact. Until he comes to Grizzly 777.

Out of habit Ozzie double checks the latitude and longitude readings for her locator beacon. No change. "Duh," he says under his breath. For the fifteenth straight week, he pencils in the same old readings for Triple Seven's den on the northwest shore of Excalibur Lake in the heart of the arctic barren-lands.

Then he sees it. "What's this?" says Ozzie, tipping back his ball cap. His finger plods across the screen below a row of flash-ing numbers indicating a change since yesterday. His finger halts abruptly, then taps the screen like a determined woodpecker. For a hibernating grizzly, all her life signs seem fired up. Heart rate, breathing, temperature. Most puzzling of all are the rhythmic jumps in muscle activity. "What the . . . ?"

Then he gets it. He hastily scribbles down Triple Seven's life-sign data, then leans back in his chair with enough speed to accidentally knock it over. He does a parachute roll on the floor, gets up without missing a beat, then bolts down the hall to his boss's office. "Hey, Vicky!" he roars, waving his field book ahead of him. "Check this out. Triple Seven's going into labor!"

The collared bear sleeps in her frozen den. The only sign of life is a faint quivering of her nostrils and the gentle heaving of her great chest. Her breathing is silent but deep. She inhales in long-drawn-out stretches, pauses for a timeless moment, then exhales a soft surge of wind. Midwinter moonlight filters through a slight thinning in the cementlike snow that plugs the mouth of the birthing den.

The big bear stirs. Her immense mass of muscle, bone, and fur begins to twitch and tremble. Her sleep becomes fitful, her breaths more labored, now coming in short pants. She feels a tightness in the muscles below her stomach. Her own heartbeat rings in her ears.

For the first time in three and a half months, the bear opens her small eyes to the den's gray-blue mist. She blinks hard. Her skull feels heavy and cold, as if packed tightly with wet sand. A dull throb pounds the back of her eyes, and her muscles are as stiff as the frozen ground all around her. Her veins feel filled with liquid lead, and her nostrils twitch to the smell of crushed willow leaves and fresh blood. Her own blood.

The big bear discovers she is no longer alone in the den.

CHAPTER 2

MOTHER LODE

When first born, they are shapeless masses of white flesh, a little
    larger than mice; their claws alone being prominent. The
    mother then licks them gradually into proper shape.
—*Pliny the Elder,* Natural History

Chief Bear Biologist Vicky Sharpe stares at the numbers in Ozzie's
field book. A petite, wiry woman with sandy red hair, she almost
disappears behind her huge oak desk, which is home to several
computers. "Do you realize what this means, Ozzie?"

"That this morning Triple Seven is one happy mom?"

"Cute. She's barely awake, Ozzie. Technically, she's still in
stage-three hibernation. No. It means that we're likely the first
biologists to witness the birth of a tundra grizzly in its natural
state."

"Electronically, of course."

"Of course." She flips the field book back to Ozzie. "The way
this technology is going, we'll soon be able to capture such events
on remote video."

"Now that's going a bit too far, don't you think? These bears
deserve *some* privacy."

"It's for their own good, Ozzie. You know that. The more data we can collect, the safer they are from humans. Especially bears that live near the diamond mine, like Triple Seven."

The newborn cub is nothing but a bloody gray lump of quivering flesh no bigger than an overgrown chipmunk. This one's a male. He weighs five hundred times less than his mother, or about as much as a small can of mushroom soup.

Already he's in trouble. His tiny hind legs are trapped under the big bear's colossal thigh, which jerks now and then, almost squeezing the life out of him minutes after being born. Another good jerk presses down on his chest, clearing the last fluid from his lungs and releasing a bubbly squeak from his pink, toothless mouth.

The great thigh lifts and a giant tongue comes to the rescue. The mother bear licks her newborn from nose to tail, then gently flips him on his back with her tongue and licks his neck and belly clean. She removes all the slimy birth fluids and membranes that, moments ago, shrouded him in a safe, warm sea. The cub's squeaks turn to birdlike chirps. She licks on, drying his thin fur, inhaling the sweet scent of her firstborn.

The swaddling tongue retreats. The cub lies alone, belly up on a bed of crushed willow leaves and blueberry twigs, an abandoned lump of life surrounded by black emptiness. With eyelids sealed tightly shut, the cub can't see his mother lying inches away.

The agony of separation ends with the cub's first sneeze. It clears his nose just enough to let in one strong message: she is near. In that instant, the scent of his mother becomes all of his world. From now on, her scent will mean security and life. Its absence will mean fear and looming death.

Like an upside down beetle finding its feet, the cub eventually manages to right himself and get up on his elbows. His fur, now dry, has the color and texture of steel wool. His weak ears are nothing but pink-rimmed tabs of flesh. His eyes are no more than scrunched-up bumps. But that nose. That nose. Already it rules his senses, steering the cub unerringly toward the wonder-filled world of his mother.

With each groping step the cub waves his spindly legs out in front as if clearing an invisible path. His head wobbles from side to side like that of a loosely held puppet.

He's learning to sniff. Her scent gets stronger. His mournful chirps rise. He's learning to whine. Finally he stumbles into her thick, soft coat. He nuzzles forward awkwardly, running his nose through her luxurious fur, poking it with his head, finding it has depths and depths and layers and layers. Now secure, the little bear falls headlong into sleep.

The deep contentment of sleeping in this furry haven soon gives way to a new, more powerful craving that overwhelms the newborn cub. He smacks his lips, frantically wiggles his puny tongue, then lets out a banshee scream. Only milk will calm him now. He doesn't know exactly where to find it, but instinct tells him it's somewhere up there.

With claws already nimble enough to grip, he climbs up his mother's mountainous leg and launches himself onto a rolling sea of fur. The fur is thinner here on her belly and a wonderful warmth flows into the podgy pads of his feet.

The craving takes hold of his ratlike body and shoves him forward. Which way? He plods south, across the furry sea. His legs swing wide in jerky swimming motions. The warmth decreases.

With great effort and squealing, he twists around and wobbles west, navigating over wave after wave of thickening fur. Cooler still. More squeals. He snags a forepaw on a shoal of matted fur. It takes all his miniscule might to wrench it free. He twists again and plods north. The waves subside. The fur gets thinner, the heat greater. He soon feels naked bearskin underfoot, almost sizzling hot.

Blind as a bat and barely able to walk, the staggering cub zeros in on his first meal, migrating along a furry trail blazed by ever-increasing heat. This route was first navigated twenty million years ago by distant ancestors belonging to the clan of the Dawn Bear. Now imprinted on every cell of his body, they steer him to the genetically promised shore. He closes the gap with a few fishlike wiggles and moors himself onto the snug harbor of his mother's nipple.

No sooner does the cub latch on with his eager mouth than a great tremor unleashes violent waves over the surrounding sea. He clamps down hard with all his gums and claws. The tremor passes. But before he can taste a drop of life-giving milk another tremor hits, this one powerful enough to wrench him loose from his moorings and send him tumbling back onto the heaving sea of fur.

The tremors get stronger, faster. Call it a bearquake. The cub hangs on for dear life, too frightened even to chirp. From somewhere far away comes the sound of hot, heavy breathing.

The tremors stop. The cub blurts out a few pathetic squeaks, then picks up the heat trail once again. He's already familiar with the thermal signposts along the way and finds another nipple in half the time of his first journey. Thirst and hunger, fear and confusion all vanish with the first few swallows of warm milk. A fifteen-minute feed inflates his scrawny body into a pleasantly plump balloon.

Moments later, the cub is rudely awakened by the raking of tiny claws across his face. Then he feels a small mouth fasten onto his nose and start sucking. Another cub, a female slightly smaller than him, is desperately looking for a drink. The male cub is still latched onto the nipple and is in no mood to share it with his newborn sister. He unclamps for a moment, shaking his nose free. The two cubs, invisible to each other, solidly bump heads. The male makes a new scratchy sound. He's learning to growl.

The female cub does not go away. She hangs around the male, trying to suck on one ear, then the other, then getting a mouthful of his claws. Another male cub soon shows up and starts climbing all over the first male's head. The bunch of them quickly turn into a squealing mass of loose legs and flailing claws, and nobody manages to get a decent drink.

Over the next few days the three cubs discover that there are five other nipples to choose from. In the meantime, between bouts of sleeping, feeding, and fighting, they stake out their claims on the furry frontier that is their mother.

The only thing Benji doesn't like about his attic room is the gargoyle. The Gloss mansion is so old that it has dozens strung along its eaves. The creature guarding Benji's window has the upper body of a woman with snakelike hair, long fangs, and enormous breasts. She crouches on thick, bearlike legs that end in a wicked set of stone claws. His mother used to call it the she-bear.

When Benji was four, he used to dare himself to look at her. He'd sneak up the attic stairs, slowly swing open the window, then back out with his bum on the window ledge and eyes scrunched shut. On the count of three—sometimes it took awhile—he'd open them wide. Like laser beams, the she-bear's stone eyes met his. They stared down on him with a mysterious mix of tenderness and terror. Once Benji almost fell to the street, so shaken was he by the power of her gaze. His mother, who had tiptoed near so as not to startle him, caught Benji by the ankle on his way down.

After that, a large padlock on the attic door barred little Benji from any more secret visits with the she-bear. But that didn't stop her from invading his sleep, even ten years later.

Instead of getting ready for the trip to Arizona with his father, Benji has fallen back into a fitful sleep. Now the she-bear is on his heels again, this time chasing him across a field of boulders. Benji's legs feel like cement. Each step takes forever. Fire burns his back. It's the she-bear's breath.

The cave! He must run for the cave. Benji slips on the wet stones. His body crumples. He claws himself forward as a shadow swallows him. Then he's in the cave, safe at last.

But the cave has no floor. Benji falls. The she-bear falls. They tumble together down a well of icy darkness. . . .

His father's limousine honks far below Benji's attic window and pulls him from the darkness.

SPRING

CHAPTER 3

LIFT-OFF

A grizzly bear has a good memory. If somebody gives it a rough
time, he remembers it for a long time.
—*Harry Simpson, Native Elder*

May 15. The helicopter pad at Saber Diamond Mine.

"Are you listening, kid?" asks the pilot.

Benji shoots him the fake paying-attention look he gives to
teachers when they catch him daydreaming. "Yup," he says.

Benji's father, a stout, balding man in a gray business suit, pokes
him with his elbow. "Pay attention, son, or you might get your
head chopped off."

Standing beside the helicopter is a slim Inuk wearing a sealskin
vest over a blue flight suit with the name *Siku* stitched on one
pocket. He spits out a tattered toothpick and lifts his mirror sunglasses to look Benji right in the eye. "Look, I don't care *whose* kid
you are. Nobody flies with me without passing chopper safety. You
lose your head, I lose my job."

"I'm listening," Benji mutters, kicking the gravel at his feet.
He barely caught a word of Siku's helicopter safety talk. The

whole time, he'd been staring at the first interesting thing he's seen since flying from San Francisco to another stupid mine: a helicopter. He's positive that whoever painted this machine had an insect in mind. Its snub-nosed head and arching thorax are gleaming black. Its long tail is striped yellow like a giant stinging wasp. Hanging below its sleek insect body is a pair of orange floats that let this creature set down anywhere on land, water, or snow. The main rotor's five silver blades droop silent and still over the crouching beast. Its call sign: CF-YEB. Yankee Echo Bravo, thinks Benji. Cool.

"Okay then," says Siku, "where did I tell you the fire extinguisher is stored?"

After one quick look at Siku's helicopter, Benji can tell him that it's a Hughes 530-F built in Mesa, Arizona, around 1990. He can tell him that it's got a 430 horsepower engine with a top speed of 180 miles an hour. He knows Siku could fly this thing upside down if he wanted to. But, because he wasn't listening, Benji can only guess the location of the fire extinguisher. He twiddles the diamond stud in his eyebrow. "Ah . . . in the rear cargo hatch?"

Siku frowns. "Not much good back there if a fire breaks out in the cabin."

Benji shrugs and rubs a thumb through his spiked blond hair. His father pokes him in the ribs again. I bet *you* don't know either, he thinks. But Benji's glad to finally get some free time with his father, even if it is at a mine, so he doesn't say anything.

"Looks like we'll have to start *all* over," says Siku.

Yeah, yeah. Band-Aids and barf bags, thinks Benji on his second time through the safety talk. Can't you just show me how to *fly* this thing?

Before climbing aboard, Siku adds, "And never forget," he says, pointing to the main rotor, "that bites." He points to the engine exhaust vent. "That burns." Then to the tail rotor. "That chews."

"Got that?" asks Benji's father as he steps hesitantly toward the helicopter.

"Sure, Dad," says Benji, racing for the front passenger door. Just as he buckles up Benji sees a mud-spattered pickup truck skid to a stop beside the helicopter. A big hairy guy jumps out and walks over to Benji's window. He gives Benji a curious look, waves a couple of fingers at his dad in the back seat, then reaches for something in his pack. "Marshmallow, kid?" the man asks, offering a fresh bag of Jumbo-Puffs as if to trade Benji for the best seat in the helicopter.

Before he can think of what to say, Benji sees a small woman run around to Siku's window. "What's going on here?" she says. "We had this chopper booked for nine o'clock. We've got to find Triple Seven's den. She may be with cubs and—" She spots Benji. "Hey! What's a kid doing in camp, let alone in *my* seat?"

Where's the fire, lady? thinks Benji. We're just going for a little joyride.

Siku points to the back seat.

Benji's father sticks his hand out the window toward the woman. "Gloss, ma'am. Ralph Gloss. Mine owner. And this is my son, Benji."

The woman covers her mouth and limply shakes his hand. "Oh . . . ah . . . Dr. Vicky Sharpe. Chief bear biologist. I didn't know it was . . ."

"That's all right," says Gloss. "I know you're very busy, baggin' bears and all. Heh-heh. My son is very interested in aircraft and has never been up in one of these babies."

Oh, so it's all my fault, thinks Benji.

Gloss unbuckles his seat belt. "Here, take my seat," he says, sounding relieved. "You go about your bear business. Benji'll stay out of your way."

"But Dad! You promised that *this* time you'd come with—"

"That's all right, son. These people have work to do, and I really should get back to my meetings."

He squeezes out the tiny door, straightens his tie, and musters a half-cheery wave to his son. Benji stares blankly at the dials on Siku's dashboard. He can hear his dad chatting up the biologists.

"You a bear bagger, too, son?" he asks the hairy guy.

"Ozzie's the name, sir. Bear baggin's the game. You pay us to keep an eye on your bears."

"I'll say. We dumped over a million bucks into your bear program last year alone."

That's peanuts to you, Pop, thinks Benji.

"Those satellite collars *are* expensive," says Vicky, "but you wouldn't believe the data that's pouring in. We've got more than fifty bears collared, and we can monitor their movements twenty-four hours a day. We're learning where they den, what they eat, how far they—"

"Just keep them critters out of my mine," says Gloss. "We've got enough trouble mining diamonds in this frozen wasteland without them getting in our way."

"Yes, sir," says Vicky as Gloss turns his back and hustles across the gravel runway. Benji looks up just as his father disappears into a red trailer. More meetings, more baby-sitters, he thinks. Some holiday.

Ozzie taps him on the shoulder as he climbs into the back seat. "Welcome aboard, Benji." He hands him a headset. "This machine's a real ear-popper. Put this on, or you may never hear your father's sweet voice again."

Vicky squishes in beside Ozzie. "Enjoy the view, kid," she grunts. "Your dad's paying for it."

Mixed-up thoughts of his father vanish with the first whine of the helicopter's turbine engine. All the dials light up. Flashing rotors bite the air. The chopper throbs with raw power. "Swe-e-e-e-t machine," he says, though no one hears him above the roar.

Just before lift-off, Benji spots a small animal whip out from under one of the floats. It sprints across the runway and makes a beeline for a long plywood building labeled *Cook Shack*. He turns to Ozzie. "You got rats up here?"

Ozzie shrugs and points to the microphone on Benji's headset. Benji swings it in front of his lips. "Was that a rat?"

"Arctic ground squirrel," says Ozzie. "I have to speak to our cook about feeding wild animals."

"Yeah," pipes in Siku, "and while you're at it, tell her that if I catch her pet squirrel chewing on my floats again, it'll be squirrel porridge for breakfast."

The engine noise rises to a smoothly controlled scream. The floats do a quick, shuffling two-step on the gravel, then spring into the air. The insect takes flight. Benji pumps a fist. "All right!"

As the chopper ascends, Benji looks down through the helicopter's wide bubble window and gets a better feel for the crazy jumble of mine buildings below. On one side of the runway he sees the flight shack, a small white building with a faded orange wind sock dangling above it. Hammered onto its side is a rough spray-painted sign: WELCOME TO SABER DIAMOND MINE.

Hugging the other side of the runway are long rows of red trailers. Behind them are three shiny white domes as big as circus tents. On the mine tour yesterday, Benji saw the inside of each one. Dome One covers a mine tunnel that pokes half a mile below the tundra. Benji wouldn't go down. No way. Mine tunnels give him the creeps. Dome Two covers the production mill, where they grind up the ore and shake out the diamonds. Whoopee, he thinks. They didn't give *me* any. Inside Dome Three is a monster power plant that keeps two hundred diamond hunters working day and night, summer or winter, including Christmas and Easter. From up here, Benji sees that the whole place is surrounded by an electric fence topped with razor wire. Poor suckers, he thinks. To him this looks like a prison camp in the middle of nowhere.

Siku has lifted the chopper straight up like an elevator, taking them a hundred stories high. Benji watches the fast-shrinking mining camp. Gravel roads branch out from the camp like arms on an octopus. The biggest one leads to a giant open pit about ten football fields wide. Mammoth ore trucks rush in and out of the pit, and raise so much dust that, to Benji, it looks like they're being swallowed by a volcano. Though he can't see it through the dust, he knows that somewhere down there is what his tour guide boastfully called "the biggest power shovel on earth."

Ozzie notices Benji staring down at the pit. "Gloss Pit. Named after your dad. Supposedly one of the richest diamond deposits on earth."

Benji had heard about Gloss Lake. But Gloss *Pit?* "I thought it was a lake."

"It was," says Ozzie, "until they drained it. It's kinda hard to mine diamonds with submarines."

Benji thinks about that for a minute. "So what did they do with the fish?"

"They invited all of Siku's relatives down from the arctic coast," says Ozzie. "They netted like crazy, then hung all the fish out to dry."

"Strange party," says Siku.

"First time on the tundra, kid?" asks Ozzie.

"Yup."

"So what do you think?"

Benji looks beyond the mine's footprint to the strange arctic landscape. Rotting snow smothers everything except the camp, a few brown meadows, and a long skinny hill that snakes off to the horizon. Big boulders stick out here and there. No trees, no mountains, no nothing, thinks Benji. The naked tundra makes him feel small and vulnerable in a way he's never felt before. For the first time in his life, he feels frightened in an aircraft.

"So?" says Ozzie.

"It's different," says Benji, hoping Ozzie didn't see him shudder. "How far to the nearest shopping mall?"

"Yellowknife. Two hundred and fifty miles south."

"I can sure see why they call it the barren-lands."

"Stick around, kid," says Ozzie. "It grows on you."

"Are you *nuts?*" says Vicky, forgetting that Benji can hear everything she says through his headset. "A mine is no place for a kid."

"I wasn't thinking of the mine."

"What? Cuddle him up to some nice tundra grizzlies? We're biologists, not baby-sitters."

Siku cuts in. "Sorry, folks, but there'll be no bear cuddling this morning."

Benji feels the chopper plunge toward camp. He doesn't care. He's lost all interest in joyriding anyway.

"What are you doing, Siku?" asks Vicky. "We've got to investigate Triple Seven's den site."

"Safety first, boss," says Siku. "Pea soup dead ahead." He points to a sideways cylinder of fog rolling straight for camp. It envelopes them just as the helicopter touches down.

"Now what?" says Benji, peering through the fog to see if his father might come to meet the downed bird.

"Plan B," says Vicky. "There's always collecting work."

"Collecting what?" asks Benji.

Siku grins.

"You wouldn't believe us if we told you," says Ozzie with a chuckle.

"Ouch! Can't they pave this road?" cries Benji as his head ricochets off the ceiling of the biologists' pickup.

"You might talk to your dad about that," says Ozzie at the wheel.

"Where are you kidnapping me to?"

"We're going collecting at the end of Gloss Road. The geologists reported seeing a bear up there yesterday, and we might find some—"

"Gloss *Road?*"

"Face it, Benji. Your dad's famous. If it weren't for him, none of us would be in this arctic paradise."

Ozzie swerves to avoid a pothole. Too late.

"Ouch!"

"It's those big ore trucks. They sure chew up the road."

Between eye-scrunching bumps, Benji watches the trucks lined up to enter Gloss Pit, which is still partly draped in fog.

"There's even a bear named after him. Glossy. A big male. Wicked temper."

Vicky looks up from her field book at the name of one of her bears. "He's mean, all right. Nearly trashed our field camp last summer. But he's not as mean as Buster."

"Who?" asks Benji.

"Buster," says Ozzie. "An uncollared bear who walked right through the electric fence last week. Helped himself to a barrel of bacon grease headed for the incinerator."

"That fence must have been broken before he went through," says Vicky. "No bear could stand up to ten thousand volts."

"Every bear's different," says Ozzie.

Benji looks at Vicky. "Then what?"

"We chased him out of camp."

"With pots and pans?"

Ozzie chuckles. "He'd eat those for dessert. With a helicopter. Buster hates helicopters."

Another pothole. "Ouch! How much farther?"

"This is it," says Ozzie as he wheels the truck into a muddy pull-off. He jumps out and starts rummaging around in back. Vicky keeps her nose in her field book. Benji looks out at a moonscape of mushy snow and tombstone boulders. Leaden clouds and fog close in around them. Yuck, he thinks. What a jolly place.

"You coming, Vic?" asks Ozzie.

"You guys go ahead," she says without looking up. "I've got some notes to write up."

"We'll keep you in sight," says Ozzie. "Honk if there's trouble." He hands Benji a fluorescent orange vest and white hard hat. "You'll need these."

Benji waves them away. "Forget it. I'm not wearing that stuff."

"Camp rules, kid. Anyone working outdoors has to." He leans closer. "It's easier to find your body if a bear gets you."

"Hah."

"Your choice. Put this on or stay in the truck."

Boring, thinks Benji. Biologists are boring. "I think I'll mosey down the road and check out my dad's diamond pit."

"I wouldn't do that if I was you," says Ozzie. "Nobody goes out alone."

"More camp rules?"

"This is grizzly country. We all have to baby-sit each other. Now, are you coming or not?"

Benji reluctantly grabs the gear and jumps out. He lands right in a puddle, instantly filling both sneakers with ice water.

"Oops," says Ozzie. "Vic, can he borrow your gum boots?"

"Forget it," says Benji. "I can handle a bit of slush." The air is cold and clammy on his bare arms and he tucks in his Twisted Sister T-shirt.

Ozzie pulls a down vest out of his pack. "Take this."

"No, thanks," says Benji as he clamps the hard hat over his spiked hair and stomps off into the snow. He stops after a few steps. "Where did you say we were going?"

Ozzie points to the long, bare hill Benji saw from the air. "Up on that esker."

"That *what?*"

"That esker. It's big pile of sand and gravel dumped by a glacier thousands of years ago. That's where they saw the bear yesterday."

"You go first."

By the time Benji reaches the bald crown of the esker, his pants are soaked to the waist. He pulls a mini CD player and earphones out of his pocket and flicks on "Gotta Get Away" by the Planet Smashers. Ozzie is on his knees, looking at something on the ground. Benji ignores him, kicking pebbles over the side of the esker, until he comes over.

"You better kill that thing. You need your ears out here."

"What's there to listen to?"

"Ever hear the sound of grizzly claws clicking over boulders? Or hear them popping their jaws just before they charge?"

"I got your point," says Benji, shoving the rig back into his wet pocket. "Hey, you never told me what we're collecting."

"Not this," says Ozzie, "but it's worth a look." He points to a pile of dark brown pellets in the sand.

"Arctic raisins?" says Benji sarcastically.

"Caribou. Probably wandered through here last fall."

"Gross."

Ozzie gently lifts the branch of a low bush. "And look at this."

Benji squints at a mound of stubby brown things. "Cigarette butts?"

"Ptarmigan. Arctic chicken."

This guy's cracked, thinks Benji. "My dad *pays* you to find animal crap?"

"Only grizzly scat."

"Huh?"

"Scat, you know, dung . . . doo-doo?"

"That's disgusting."

"It's gold, Benji."

"I think you're sick."

"Honest. Nothing like a fresh, steamy scat to brighten up a bear biologist's day."

Benji rolls his eyes.

"Sometimes if we're working on a drugged bear and it won't produce for us, we'll even reach in and help ourselves," says Ozzie, thrusting his hand upward.

"Now I *know* you're sick."

"With gloves on, of course," he adds. "Stale or fresh, we'll dissect them to see exactly what a bear had for breakfast."

"So what?"

"By studying hundreds of scats you can figure out what foods they like best at different times of year."

"Not me, thanks." Now I know biology is a joke, thinks Benji. Squishing frogs. Pressing plants. And sniffing bear turds. But his dad said he pumped big bucks into bear work. "Why should a mine care less about what a bear eats?"

"Well, you don't want to build a mining road right over a bear's favorite berry patch. Whether your dad likes grizzlies or not, he has a legal duty to protect them. So he hires hotshots like Vicky to tell him how to dig up diamonds without hassling bears. I'm just her flunkie technician."

Ozzie stoops over to pick up some abandoned mining stakes. A raven drops out of the thinning fog and lands near Benji. He is about to kick a pebble at it when he hears Vicky blasting the horn. "What's with *her?*"

"Sounds serious," says Ozzie. "Let's boot it."

Just before Benji plunges back into the snow Ozzie shouts,

"Freeze!" Feeling a bit like he's in a police movie, Benji stops his foot in midair.

Ozzie yanks a plastic bag out of his vest. "Eureka!"

"What?"

"Our bear scat! You almost stepped in it."

Benji jumps backward.

Ozzie inverts the bag, shoves his hand in, and plucks up a big purple mess. "Isn't she a beauty?"

"Eee-ew."

"Still warm."

Benji bolts upright and looks over both shoulders.

"Just kidding." Ozzie seals the bag, then struggles with his pack. Vicky is leaning on the horn. "Darn zipper's stuck. I got my hands full with these stakes. Here, you take it." He tosses the scat bag to Benji, who throws his hands in the air.

"My dad could fire you for this!"

"Your dad paid a lot of money for that scat." Ozzie bounds off through the snow.

These guys are crazy, thinks Benji as he picks up the bag between two fingernails and straight-arms Ozzie's treasure back to the truck.

"Come on, come on," yells Vicky, now at the wheel.

"Present for you," says Benji, tossing the scat bag in her lap.

She admires it for a second. "Good work, Ozzie."

"Thank Benji. He found it."

"Yeah right," he says. "What's the panic?"

"Camp phoned. Buster's back," says Vicky and she floors it down the road.

At this pace, Benji decides to keep his helmet on to avoid cracking his head open on the truck ceiling. Just past the open pit, they come over a hill and almost crash into a yellow, three-story building on wheels.

"Whoa, baby!" exclaims Benji as Vicky slams on the brakes. "Now *that's* a truck!" He leans forward to study the truck's front grill and humongous tires. "Caterpillar 793-A. Sucks back sixty gallons of fuel an hour. Holds about 300 tons of blown-up rock."

Ozzie raises his eyebrows. "Into ore trucks, too, eh? Seen a few mines?"

"A few," he says, slouching back in his seat. "It's my dad's idea of a holiday, lugging me around the world to look at big holes in the ground."

"Road hog!" yells Vicky. "Don't you know there's a bear in camp?"

"Easy, Vicky," says Ozzie. "There's a pull-out right behind us. These guys own the road. Let him pass."

By the time they get back to camp, Siku has the chopper powered up. Vicky reluctantly agrees to take Benji, who is once again primed to fly. He piles in the back with Ozzie, and in seconds they are streaking over the camp.

"Where was he last seen?" Vicky asks Siku.

"Sniffing around where he bust through last time. They fired a couple bear bangers, and he took off over the hill."

"How do they know it was Buster?"

"Huge. Dark. Same scarred-up face."

"There!" says Ozzie. "At nine o'clock."

Benji leans almost into Ozzie's lap to see a grizzly bear running full tilt through the mushy snow. "Big sucker!"

"The biggest," says Ozzie.

Over his headset Benji hears Vicky commanding the chase. "Lower, Siku. Faster. Let him feel your wind at his back."

The helicopter plunges toward the bear. It follows his every move, rocking and rolling through the air like a sports car on a twisty track. The bear gallops through deep snow and over jagged boulders with the ease of a deer skipping through a meadow. To Benji, the chase goes on for an awfully long time, but it ends abruptly when the bear loses his footing and stumbles headfirst into a rock. "Yikes! Is he okay?"

"He's tough," says Ozzie.

Buster shakes his great head. The helicopter moves closer, almost grazing the bear's rump with its floats. Benji glimpses ugly scars on his muzzle and shoulders. The bear springs to a stand and takes a swipe at the helicopter with his mighty foreclaws.

Benji recoils in his seat. Buster's flashing claws seem to reach through the helicopter and tear open an old wound in Benji's heart. The sight triggers bizarre memories that barge into his brain. Stone claws . . . his mother's scream . . . falling into darkness . . . Benji shuts his eyes.

"Easy on my floats, Buster!" says Siku.

Benji opens his eyes to see Siku pull the chopper's nose away from Buster's claws just in time.

"Get back on him," says Vicky and the high-speed chase resumes. "Ozzie, do you think you could dart Buster at this speed? I'd sure like to get a satellite collar on him."

Benji sees Ozzie look up from the fleeing bear with wide eyes. "It's too risky, Vicky. It could get ugly if he comes storming back to camp half-corked on our tranquilizer. Besides, haven't you collared enough bears up here?"

"It's important that we closely monitor the movements of problem bears."

Ozzie shakes his head. "You can't monitor the movements of a dead bear. Which is what he'll be if he comes back a third time. You said it yourself: three strikes and you're out."

Benji sees Buster stumble again and flop helplessly into a deep puddle of meltwater. His mind grapples with the riddle of this beast. The towering monster that raked his soul moments ago is now a defenseless prey, pinned down by a helicopter. "Man!" says Benji. "I thought you said you were paid to protect these bears, not fly helicopters up their—"

Ozzie looks right at him. "The kindest thing we can do for that bear is scare him out of his wits so he'll never come back."

"Seems weird to me."

"A fed bear's a dead bear, Benji. We're teaching Buster a lesson here. Your dad's mine is a death trap for nosy bears, not a candy store."

CHAPTER 4

REBIRTH

We have only a word, "smell," to include the whole range of
delicate thrills which murmur in the nose of the animal night
and day, summoning, warning, inciting and repelling.
—Kenneth Grahame, Wind and the Willows

I thought that kid would never leave," says Vicky as she bangs away
on her computer in the environmental trailer at Saber Mine.

"He hasn't."

"Why not?"

"Siku tells me there's a blizzard warning, and they're not letting
any planes out. Not even Gloss's private jet."

"Benji should never have come with us. How are we supposed
to do any work with a city slicker punk leeching on to us?"

"Good investment, I think," says Ozzie.

Vicky looks up from her computer. "How so?"

"It's not every kid who gets a bird's-eye view of a wild grizzly
galloping across the barren-lands. Buster put on a good show for
him, swinging his claws at the chopper like that. Keep Gloss's kid
happy, Gloss is happy, and you're happy 'cause he doesn't ax your
money-sucking bear program."

Vicky nods slightly. "He's threatened to do that more than once."

"Can't hurt, Vic. I'll work on the kid. Who knows? He might even help you find Triple Seven and her cubs."

"Fat chance."

"That is, if Buster doesn't find them first."

It's the smell that wakes her up. A thick, skunky smell—one the mother bear could ignore if it weren't for the cubs. Her nose is on the move long before her eyes. She hears a dull thump directly above the den, then a scratching noise near the den's mouth.

She opens her eyes and peers down the tunnel to the snow-packed entrance. The den brightens as the scratching and digging continue. A dim, gray light gives way to a bluish glow, then bright white. That stench fills the den.

The cubs start whining up a storm. Without taking her eyes off the brightening tunnel, their mother stuffs them behind her with a quick sweep of both forelegs.

The scratching stops. For a moment, so does the whining. The mother bear raises a pawful of claws. She hears a grunt, a hiss, then . . . nothing. A shadow moves across the paper-thin layer of snow still plugging the den. Then it quickly pulls back, and sunlight floods the snowy veil.

The odor fades. The cubs whimper. Their mother barely breathes. She keeps her paw raised and ready.

Just as the cubs start squeezing around her, the bandit face of a wolverine bursts into the den. A shower of sharp frost crystals flies into the bear's eyes, and she's temporarily blinded. But her claws find their mark on the muzzle of the intruder, slashing it deeply. The wolverine struggles free and retreats as fast as it attacked.

The big bear casually sniffs her bloodied paw before licking it clean. The lingering scent tells her the invader was an immature male, likely hungry for the flesh of bear cub.

A wide shaft of sunlight reaches into the den. The cubs rub their eyes and whine. For them, it is like a second birth, a widening of the earth's womb, a passage through which they must now travel into another strange new world. The sunlight pours in with a river of scents that teases the cubs' nostrils, even while they whimper, and it lures them toward the den mouth. They stumble over the mountainous mass of their mother.

Unlike her cubs, she is in no hurry to go anywhere. She interrupts their wobbling march with a thorough tongue bath, as if preparing them for their world debut.

She starts on the biggest one, a male. She knows she can't pin this cub down for long. He half closes his eyes as his mother's tongue licks backward over the top of his head and down his long, upturned muzzle. At twenty-six pounds, he weighs a third more than his sister and twice as much as his little brother.

Though each cub was born on the same day, three and a half months later they are now vastly different. Since birth, the best squabbler got the most milk. The success of the big male's many fights is recorded not only in his size but in the battle scars of his siblings. The female cub has several thin scars running down her muzzle. The runt male is more badly scarred and has a fresh wound on his upper lip, inflicted by the needle-sharp teeth of his scarless brother.

The big male cub is first out. He swats his eyes as if wiping away the dazzling glare of sun and snow. He squints all around. The den is perched near the top of an esker. Above it is a thick eyebrow of dwarf birch and willow shrubs still choked with snow. The den faces directly into the midday sun, and the cub is almost knocked over by the brightness and newness of it all.

He takes a few clumsy steps and looks over the edge of the rubble pile made when his mother dug the den last fall. The esker falls away at a dizzying angle, ending in a clump of shrubs along a frozen lakeshore. Everything else is white except for the rubble at his feet, the odd boulder sticking out of the snow, and the bald crown of the esker.

The cub hears a strange laughing sound above and timidly cocks his head up to see a loose V of snow geese. He hears a low, throaty *kar-kee-karrrr*, then leaps sideways as a rock ptarmigan flaps right past his head. He lands on his back and is ambushed by his sister. They bat each other's faces and tug on their ears. They lock jaws and wrestle each other to the ground. The runt male dives in, starting a new round of grab, twist, and tumble. The cubs wrestle in silence except for snakelike hissing sounds that escape through their black button noses.

The games end when their mother thrusts her head out of the den. They half run, half fall toward her, then climb over her face. She is trapped for a second as the blocky satellite transmitter on her collar catches the hard snow rimming the den mouth. One good boost and she emerges like a giant breaking free from its chains.

The cubs fall in helpless heaps behind her. They are starved and turn up the volume on their whines. The big male climbs onto her back as she waddles stiffly into the light. The other two hang on like a pair of sidesaddles even while she stretches her powerful limbs.

She digs her massive front claws into the mud, straightens her forelegs, and thrusts her bum into the air. Then she teeters the other way, pulling her head and chest forward into an arc as if offering greetings to the sun. It will take her several days to undo the tangled knots and aching kinks in her muscles after seven months of sleeping in a ball.

She scratches her satellite collar with her hind paw, just like a dog with a bad case of fleas. Then, while her cubs bawl, she stands, motionless and silent, bringing all her concentration to the tip of her nose.

Her nostrils twist in excitement. She closes her eyes for a moment, then moves her head from side to side like a cobra. With the precision of a surgeon's knife, she dissects the whispering breeze into its component scents.

She sniffs a great sniff. Some scents are thin, others thick. Some scents speckle the air currents like buckshot; others hover like colorful ribbons. Some are fresh and strong, others old and blurry. She can read them all. *Sniff.* In comes the sweet smell of dwarf birch, the ashy, gunpowder smell of sunbaked boulders, the heavy odor of red fox. Swinging her head, she sniffs again. Now it's the bitter smell of raven. She lowers her head. *Sniff.* In rush the prickly fragrances of smaller creatures: arctic hare, vole, and lemming. *Sniff.* And that skunky odor of the wolverine.

The big male cub, saddled high on his mother's hump, chomps angrily on her collar. The other two still hang from her side. They've had quite enough of this sniffing business. These scents mean nothing to them, and by now they are frantic with hunger. And fear. The puzzling blare of new smells, sights, and sounds has them thoroughly befuddled. They crave the safety and security that only a good suckle can give.

Finally—*finally*—she snaps out of her sniffing spell and turns her head toward her cubs. The two smaller cubs run around to her nose, pushing on it as if to knock her backward into a nursing position. Left out of the action for a moment, the big male plops to the ground and scatters his siblings with a few shrill growls.

The mother rears up, pivots on her heels, and collapses onto her back. She hardly hits the ground before her cubs land on the vast expanse of her hairy bosom and latch onto a nipple. As hungry and happy as they are, everyone knows this is no time to break the long-established rules of nursing: the big male gets all three nipples on his mother's right; the other three are shared between his sister and the runt.

The air fills with a peculiar chuckling noise, like the sound your finger makes when rubbed quickly over a wet balloon. It's the music of nursing bruins. They suck and chuckle, chuckle and suck until a white froth of milk rings each nipple. With tummies swollen round, the cubs gallop and buck like miniature ponies over their mother's cinnamon curls.

She suddenly lifts her nose to some faint new scent in the wind. Her black lips close, the lower one protruding slightly, and she sniffs. The caves and passageways in her muzzle—a hundred times more sensitive than ours—are bathed in an odor too weak for any other animal to detect. She opens her mouth, releasing a burst of air, then closes it to sniff again. She huffs and puffs like this until she identifies the scent: wolf, immature male. The scent is too old and faraway to be of concern, but she rolls over anyway, spilling a jumble of squealing cubs. She waddles stiff-legged down the esker toward the frozen lake. The round-bellied cubs wobble in a loose group behind her, disappearing one after another into the deep bowls of snow made by her giant paws.

The biggest cub soon tires of falling into his mother's tracks and sets off on his own. The old, grainy snow supports his weight, and he runs to catch up. Just before reaching her, he trips, rolls right past her, and starts sliding across the snow on his belly like a kamikaze starfish. The cub crashes to a halt in a clump of shrubs below the esker. His anguished yelps send his mother sailing down the slope straight for him.

Her tobogganing style is much more sophisticated. She slides bum first with her rear legs pointing skyward. She controls her descent by reaching behind and using her foreclaws as brakes and rudder in the snow—a technique learned from her mother fourteen springs ago. Just before her 450-pound bulk crashes into the cub, she rams her right paw into the snow and comes to a perfect, curving stop. The big bear flips effortlessly to her feet and throws off a small hill of snow with a shrug and shake.

Upslope, the other two cubs still struggle through her tracks. As they pop in and out of view, she hears their cries, now ear-piercing as they emerge from one track, now muffled as they fall into another. To them, the end of the world arrived when their mother deserted them to go tobogganing.

She woofs at them. The stranded cubs halt. She woofs again, louder. They stand there bawling, feeding each other's misery.

Their big brother, meanwhile, has untangled himself from the bushes. He stumbles over to reclaim his mother's back and discovers how to hang on extra tight by hooking his claws under her satellite collar. She ignores him woofing away at his siblings, whose misery increases by the second. They're in no mood for tobogganing. And their mother has no time for coaxing.

Something else is in the wind. Spilling over the esker is a skunky scent that makes her nostrils quiver. She slams her forepaws into the snow, then springs to a full stand. The large male cub, still clamped to her collar, dangles almost six feet off the ground, too startled to make a peep.

The big bear peers upslope. She sees a flash of brown and yellow fur. It's that young wolverine again, the one that invaded their den. She watches him advance, head down, in a winding trot. In a moment he will be right above the stranded cubs. He'll probably see them. For sure he'll hear them.

An emergency gate opens in the big bear's brain, releasing a surge of adrenaline through her body. Her massive legs, still burdened by the sloth of hibernation, explode into motion. The male cub clutches her collar like a rookie rodeo rider, his rear end flopping wildly back and forth with every bound she makes. *Yeehaw!* She makes the fifty-yard trip up the steep, snowbound esker in four seconds—less time than it took her to slide down.

By the time the wolverine lifts its chunky head, the big bear is already standing over her cubs, half smothering them in snow.

With the breeze at his back and sun in his face, the wolverine receives no clues about the commotion that's occurred below him. He sits on his haunches and shades his eyes with a raised paw much like a sea captain. Against the glare of sun and snow, he picks out the silhouette of the grizzly that raked his nose. Recognizing the true landlord of this esker, he flashes his hyena teeth at the bear, lets out a weak hiss and turns tail for a fast retreat.

Now it's the big male cub's turn to bawl. As the mother bear waits for the wolverine stench to thin out, the other two cubs grab this chance for a quick slurp at the ceiling of nipples above them.

Their mother holds her ground for a while, then heads straight for the den, the two young cubs trundling behind. The cub on her back, still shook up and bawling, is knocked off when she enters the den. He promptly gets up and attacks the runt male, batting his muzzle and chewing his ears. The female cub dives into the fray, belly flopping onto her brothers. Amid husky growls, they claw and cuff and chase one another until two giant arms draw the whole tussling lot of them back into the den.

A few hours later, Ozzie stands alone on the plywood deck of the cook shack, enjoying an after-dinner blizzard. The weather has turned from sweet to sour. A fierce north wind smothers the mining camp in a river of driving snow. Ozzie can't see much beyond his nose. Lousy tracking tomorrow, he thinks. Everything'll be cemented over with snow. He could use a day off. Then he remembers his surprise for Benji: to take him bear hunting in the Beaver.

CHAPTER 5

BEAR HUNT

I know she's down there somewhere. She's gotta be.
—*Vivian Banci, Bear Biologist*

The next day, Benji sits alone in the Saber Mine cafeteria pushing squashed peas around his plate. With the metallic techno-beat of Prozzäc jangling his earphones, he doesn't hear Ozzie come in. The bench shakes, and he looks up to see Ozzie sitting beside him, casually picking bits of sauerkraut out of his beard. Gross. It's the scat-man, thinks Benji.

Ozzie nods and mutters something.

Benji yanks out his earphones. "What?"

"There's still some lime Jell-O left."

"Forget it. How do you survive on this prison food?"

"I beef up my diet with berries and roots. You know, bear chow?" Ozzie pulls out a marshmallow. "Oh, and these." He tosses it onto Benji's plate. Benji promptly flicks it away like a hockey puck.

"So your holiday got extended?"

"Stupid blizzard yesterday."

"And this morning?"

"More meetings. What else?"

"I just bumped into your dad. Tells me you can join us on today's bear hunt."

The image of Buster's chewed-up face and flashing claws pops into Benji's head. Opposing currents of fear and fascination tug at his heart. Seeing that bear revealed a window in him that he's unsure about looking through. Another bear encounter might let him steal a peek. He's curious and torn. If only his father would come.

"He never tells *me* anything."

"He seemed in an awful hurry."

Benji huffs.

"Seen many beavers in California?"

"I thought you were *bear* biologists."

"I mean Turbo-Beavers, the ones with propellers."

Benji straightens up. "What's wrong with the chopper?"

"It's in for repairs. Seems a wolf chewed up the pilot's seat."

"What did Sickie say?"

Ozzie laughs. "It's *See-koo,* and you're too young for me to repeat it."

"Hah."

"We can cover more ground in the Beaver. Besides, it's cheaper. Saves your dad some pennies. Interested?"

Benji ponders the alternative: a boring afternoon stuck in camp. "Sure. Time for more Buster lessons?"

"He's long gone, I hope. We're tracking Triple Seven. Vicky's darling."

Wearing that goofy hard hat and orange vest, Benji walks with Ozzie across the runway toward a mustard-colored floatplane.

Vicky is already in the copilot's seat, waving at them to hurry up. He sees Siku kick one of the little tires hanging under the floats. "You fly this thing, too?" Benji asks.

"Kid, I'll fly anything not nailed down."

"Amphibious," says Benji. "They don't make this model anymore."

"Threatened species. Just like Vicky's bears."

Minutes later they are airborne, nine miles east of the mine. Benji hears Siku's voice in his headset. "Saber Base, this is Oscar Papa Zulu. Do you copy? OPZ to Saber. Do you copy?"

"Saber here. What's your status, Siku?"

"We're dropping down to buzz Excalibur Lake. Looking for a bear den. It's low-level work, so we'll be out of touch for a bit."

"Roger, OPZ. Losing radio contact during low-level survey. Give us a shout when you're out of the ditch."

"Ten-four. Oscar Papa Zulu clear."

Benji looks out his rear bubble window. The sky is white. The ground is white. After the blizzard, everything is white except for a few shrubs and boulders. Viewing this vast lifeless world, Benji again feels smaller than an ant.

"Down there, Siku" says Vicky, pointing to a high, snakelike hill.

"Who this time?"

"Triple Seven. The data from her satellite collar suggests she busted out yesterday."

Siku nods without looking at her.

"We think she's with cubs."

Another nod.

Siku drops the plane's nose until Benji sees snow-caked tundra filling the front windshield. Cowboy, he thinks.

"Low enough for you?" asks Siku.

Vicky glances up from her field book. "Okay. Level off."

Benji sees white above, white below. "How could you find anything down there?"

"Just watch me," says Vicky. "We have the technology. Siku, here are Triple Seven's coordinates. Latitude sixty-six degrees, four minutes, six seconds north. . . ."

Benji sees Siku's black-gloved thumb punch some tiny gray buttons on the dashboard. "What's all that about?" he asks Ozzie.

"GPS."

"Huh?"

"Global Positioning System. It lets us lock on to the exact spot where the satellite tells us a bear should be."

"Cool." Benji has a soft spot for high-tech gizmos.

Vicky races on. "Longitude a hundred and fifteen degrees. . . ."

"Wait a second," says Siku. *Punch, punch.* "Okay, proceed."

"Longitude a hundred and fifteen degrees, zero minutes, nine seconds west."

Punch. "GPS locked on, boss."

Ozzie taps Benji on the shoulder. "The den will probably be out your window. They like to build them on the sunny side. Keep an eye out for tracks, scats, digs, bedding areas, caribou kills—anything to say a bear's been around. That blizzard kinda messed things up, but you might get lucky."

"You guys paying me for this?"

"No. You're paying us. Here comes the esker. Start lookin'."

Benji sees Vicky bob her head up and down as she sweeps the white hills for bear signs. He tries this himself but only gets a headache.

"Where is she?" says Vicky.

Siku glances at the GPS target indicator. "Whoops. Looks like we just flew over her."

Without a word, Vicky spins her index finger near Siku's nose. He hauls back on the steering wheel and heaves the plane into a stiff left-hand turn. Canned peas sink like stones to the pit of Benji's stomach.

"This visibility sucks," Vicky mutters.

"What?" says Siku.

"This sucks! I can't see anything down there. What's our altitude?"

"We don't have any. We're as low as she'll go. Any lower and you'll need a snowmobile . . . or an ambulance." Siku checks the GPS. "Okay. Here comes your bear den." The esker slides below them at a hundred miles an hour. "It should be . . . right . . . down . . . *there!*"

To Benji, the wind-whipped snowdrifts coating the esker look like meringue on a lemon pie. The first living thing he sees is a big white bird rocketing up from a boulder.

"Ptarmigan," says Ozzie before Benji gets a chance to ask.

"Maybe your satellite had a bad day," says Siku.

Vicky ignores him, spinning her finger. Again the plane lurches to the left.

Again the peas sink in Benji's stomach. "Puke."

"Not here, please," says Ozzie.

Like the pendulum on a clock, the plane swoops back and forth over the esker. Nine times they make a hopeful pass over the phantom bear den. At the start of the tenth pass, Benji closes his eyes, trying hard not to throw up. A debate starts up in his headset.

"Forget it, Vic," says Ozzie.

"What?"

"Forget it, Vicky. Triple Seven's either snowed in or long gone."

"The satellite says she's down there. She's been moving about, and I don't want to lose her."

"We'll never lose her as long as she's wearing that collar."

"You know how good she is at hiding."

"Why don't we let the snow melt a bit, then come back in the chopper?"

There is a long pause. Benji almost falls asleep. Finally Vicky says, "Sounds good, Ozzie. Glad I thought of it. One more pass and we'll head back to Saber camp. Did you get that, Siku?"

"Roger."

"As low as legal, okay?"

"It's your show."

The only bears Benji sees that day are in his dreams on the flight back to camp. Something about bear cubs playing in the snow.

Inside the grizzly den, the rattle of the plane's engine shakes loose a scattering of frost crystals from the frozen ceiling. The cubs sleep soundly. Not far above their heads, a strange thunder tears the fabric of the sky. The mother bear trembles while slipping into a dream triggered by the memory of that sound.

The flickering dream deepens. Its images take shape. It now possesses the bear completely.

Her jaw clicks. Her long slender foreclaws gently rake the air. Her stomach squeezes in on itself. She is eating blueberries. There are so many berries that she can lie flat on her belly with elbows in the sand and push herself from bush to bush with only a short nudge of her hind feet.

The sandy esker is purple with berries. She combs the branches with her teeth and sweeps huge clawfuls of sweet berries into her mouth. She eats and eats until her face and chest are streaked with berry juice. She pushes herself forward, wriggling on and on, over a boundless blueberry sea.

Something breaks the spell and makes her stop midchew. The bear's cottonball ears jump to attention, then fold backward in retreat. A low, pounding, insect noise shatters the sky behind her, but a thick heaviness prevents her from turning to look at the thing making the noise. She can hardly breathe.

Suddenly, she is on her feet, galloping over the blueberries, running for her life. The sound is now more above her than behind and has changed into a shrill whine that shudders through her skull. She keeps running until a cone of fiercely whirling air drops from the sky, imprisoning her in confusion. She halts. The wind wraps around her like invisible arms, flattening the bushes, mashing her thick fur. Loose pebbles and blueberries bounce madly away in every direction.

With great effort, the bear finally manages to steal a glance over her shoulder. She sees three humans perched inside the belly of a black helicopter. One of them leans out, resting something long and shiny against an open window.

Again she breaks into a run. The whirling funnel of wind keeps pace. Above the scream of the helicopter comes a sharp crack, then another. Puffs of dirt fly up in her face and she spins around into the swirling sand. A final crack and some stinging thing pierces her shoulder.

The dream blurs. She is running, tripping over her legs, falling, rolling to a stop.

The helicopter is down. It screams on. Two humans slowly walk toward her. Slower . . . and . . . slower. Their shapes melt into each other, into the sky. Everything blends into a wet smear of blue, green, and purple. Blurring . . . blurring. It's as if she is watching the scene from underwater—and she's sinking fast.

Her nostrils flare. That scent is all around. So strong. That dreaded human scent. Salt, oil, plastic, smoke. Human hands are on her ears, around her neck, in her mouth. They squeeze her lips and tug at her teeth. She tries in vain to snap off the intruding fingers. They probe her insides from behind, shaking her bowels loose. She manages a weak, raspy growl.

Defeated, she closes her dream eyes and falls into a rapid pant. The sound goes away. The dream ends.

CHAPTER 6

CLAIM-STAKING

Typically, once a bear claims a carcass, nothing
can drive it away except a larger bear.
—*Wayne Lynch*, Bears

A week after the blizzard, the bears finally leave the den. The snow
is rotten under their paws. Most has collapsed into mush in the hot
spring sun. Many south-facing slopes are bare, heaping the air with
new scents: soggy peat moss, dead grass, last fall's cranberries.
There are slivers of open water along the shore. But the ice on
Excalibur Lake is sturdy. It stands up well, without cracks, bends,
or pops, to the slow parade of bears who follow their noses across
their domain.

The collared bear lumbers in the lead. The fur covering her legs,
paws, and shoulder hump is much darker than the rest of her frosty
blonde coat, which ripples with honeyed highlights as she walks.
First a hind leg swings forward, then, a bit later, the front leg on
the same side, then the legs on the other side follow suit, much like
a giant caterpillar.

When she breaks into a trot to reel in her wandering cubs, her
hind legs swing sideways as much as forward, giving her rear end a

clownish roll—deceptively clownish when you consider that this bear could outrun a racehorse in a blind dash.

She stops often, waiting patiently for her cubs. Sometimes she twists her head over her shoulder and grunts. Other times she just halts, squinting and sniffing indifferently.

The chocolate-colored cubs have yet to master the classic bear walk. Their legs bow out while their toes point in. Their front legs awkwardly bat the air with each step. Their hind legs carve random scribbles in the snow. They occasionally fling their little butts in the air or spring backward when spooked by their own shadows. Hesitation and fear rule every step. But they keep moving, driven forward by the magnetism of their mother and a fierce curiosity to explore this new world.

The bears march through a wiggly world of shimmering heat waves and bizarre mirages that hover above the ice. Islands float over the horizon. Clouds quiver below it. Distant boulders stretch like rubber bands into the sky.

The mother bear is suddenly parched. The cubs have been nursing more than ever, almost sucking her dry. She sweeps aside a pawful of slush and sniffs at the exposed ice. Somehow she knows it's too thick. She wanders ahead and sweeps away more slush. Another sniff. Then she raises a giant paw and slams it down— *whack*—upon the ice. One blow sends a spray of ice chunks and arctic-chilled water into her face. She buries her muzzle down the ice hole and takes a slow, deep drink. She looks up, snorts the water out of her nose and sniffs hard.

There's blood on the ice. She smells it long before she sees it. The parade abruptly changes course, stopping at a splatter of red slush. The stain is criss-crossed with the knobby tracks of raven feet.

The cubs stay clear of the blood until they see their mother take a few licks. Then they hop onto the stain, trying to claim this new prize. They chase and wrestle each other through the blood until they discover that their mother is gone. She's following a blood trail that leads straight for the lakeshore.

Her nose tells her there's been a battle between a young male wolf and a caribou cow. The blood is fresh and has the odor of both. She studies the trail. The wounded wolf appears to have dragged the caribou across the ice, making a wide, blood-smeared trail that blots out his prints.

Halfway to shore, the big bear halts to woof at her cubs. They run toward her as fast and straight as their wobbly legs can carry them. Their sharp claws give them good traction over the slush-covered ice, but they are no good as brakes. Like a bump-and-grind car crash, the cubs pile solidly into their mother's hairy rump.

The blood trail leads to a strange cluster of rock slabs that reach high into the air. The mother bear springs to a stand but can't see over the tallest of them.

The cubs watch their mother closely. The big male cub tries his mother's standing trick, but isn't so adept. He springs once and falls backward, springs twice and tumbles sideways. Then, triumphantly, he stands upright . . . for two seconds. The two smaller cubs try but teeter over like nudged bowling pins. Their mother drops to all fours and ambles toward the rocks.

Behind every slab, she expects to discover the wolf feasting on a caribou. But the blood trail goes on and on through the labyrinth of standing stones. For any wolf, injured or not, a caribou would be no small burden to lug across the lake, let alone drag through this tangled forest of rocks.

What the bear finally sees is so unexpected that she lets out a high, cublike squeal. The caribou is on her feet. Her head is down. Half of her antlers are buried in the rib cage of a black wolf. The wolf is dead. It probably died instantly when gored by the caribou. With a wolf stuck to its antlers, the caribou dragged it all this way. A long, bloody gash in her rump shows where the unlucky wolf must have clamped on but lost his grip.

Sticky white froth drips from the caribou's panting mouth. It looks at the bear with eyes so wide and fearful they are rimmed all around with white. The caribou's hind legs shake, and its chest heaves with each pant. But she musters a few sharp snorts at the bear. She stamps the bloody snow as if to defy the certainty of death now staring her in the face.

The big bear walks casually up to the caribou and finishes her off with one lightning strike to her head. The caribou's legs briefly thrash the air. Except for some whimpering from the runt male, all is silent.

Then come the ravens. They announce their intent to steal and harass with crazy croaks that echo through the rocks. Before the big bear gets a chance to sniff her first meal since October, one raven sets to work tugging on the dead wolf's eye. Another two gobble down some red snow while hopping about squawking at each other.

For now, the big bear ignores them. She starts peeling long strips of hide off the caribou's belly and swallowing them whole. But the cubs cannot resist these long-tailed playmates. They rush the ravens over and over, trying to swat them with their puny paws. With each attack, the ravens merely flit away just as a cub gets within range. This game continues until the big male cub gets so far away his mother is forced to fetch him. She finds him behind one of the taller rocks taking futile swipes at a raven.

The bird looks down on the bears with blinking eyes. It swivels its head first one way, then the other, while snapping its big hollow beak. Hoarse, gravelly sounds spout from deep in its throat. An oily, bitter smell fills the mother bear's nose. She pretends not to see the raven, then suddenly bolts to her hind feet and takes a swing at it. The bird is too quick. Not a feather is ruffled. The bear drops down and delivers a swift cuff to her cub that sends him squealing across the mushy snow.

By the time the bears get back to the kill, all three ravens have their heads buried in caribou guts. The front legs of an unborn caribou calf poke out of a slash made by the bear. Meanwhile a male arctic fox has started ripping open the wolf. The big bear lunges at the ravens while taking a sideswipe at the fox.

The fox trots a few paces away, then calmly licks blood off its front paws. The ravens hop about squawking as usual. All eyes are fixed on the bear. They watch for the slightest chance to snitch a piece of her prize.

There is no feast. Not yet. The cubs are still weeks away from eating anything solid. Except for a few slurps of blood, they eat nothing of this kill. And their mother, not long out of her den, is still in a state of walking hibernation and has little appetite. After gulping down the caribou's heart and liver, her hunger fades. She wanders into the shade of some willows and flops on her back.

The fox and ravens immediately descend on her kill. They enjoy a good feast while dodging attacks from the cubs. During one rush from the runt male, the fox wheels around and nips his paw. At the sound of his forlorn yelp, his mother merely lifts her head and yawns.

Soon it's time for a good scratch. She stands, aims her rump at the willows, then rams herself backward until she finds a trunk big enough to stand up to her feverish rubbing. She swings her butt across the trunk while making loud, contented grunts. She leans back, tilting her head skyward, exposing her whole back to a delicious scratch. Her loose, black-lipped mouth opens and closes with each twist. Tingling waves of pleasure run up her spine and into her limbs. At the edge of the willows, her cubs chase the end of a branch that swings teasingly before them in time with their mother's wiggles.

She plows deeper into the willows, determined to scratch one of her main itch targets: her satellite collar. Hanging like a dead weight around her neck, the collar and heavy transmitter box create a hot, tingling zone. For relief, she reaches up to some thick branches, draws them down to her neck, then rubs madly against them.

When the bear emerges from the willows, she sees a host of newcomers feasting on her kill: a bald eagle, two herring gulls, and another mob of ravens. Something in her snaps, and she charges the lot of them.

The gulls beat a noisy retreat while the fox steals one last bite of wolf meat, then slinks behind a snowdrift. The ravens leap into the air and line up along the highest rocks while hurling guttural abuse at the bears. The bald eagle catapults upward with a few powerful wing strokes and is soon circling high overhead.

The bear spends the next two hours burying the caribou and wolf carcasses with anything she can. First she scrapes a huge mound of snow over the animals. Then she rakes at the frozen tundra floor, ripping up grasses, moss, and earth to spread over the rising pile.

Finally, like a giant beaver, she drags in willow branches, some of which she tore off with her teeth. She chucks these on top of the meat cache like a dressing of sprouts on a salad.

In the end, she has built herself a cache that is twelve feet across and half as high. Only the tips of the caribou antlers remain exposed.

As the scent and sight of meat dwindles, and the big bear's claim is made clear—by her sitting squarely on top of it—the mob of thieving scavengers begins to scatter. The fox is seen no more. The gulls and eagle head for open water. Even some of the ravens disappear. But three remain, kicking up a fuss whenever the big bear moves a muscle.

She ignores the birds, sniffing the wind and yawning in their faces. She lazily rolls over onto her belly with her forelegs splayed out in front. She flips up one paw and licks at the snow packed between her toes. She pauses to look around for the cubs. They're asleep in a heap beside the cache. She flips up her other paw and repeats the same cleaning process. By next fall, the pads of her feet will be thick and calloused, but today they are tender from many months of disuse. While gnawing the snow from her toes, she accidentally nicks one of her pads. Blood trickles onto the snow.

The big male cub wakes and comes tripping up the mound. He sniffs the bloody snow by his mother's paw. The smell makes him whine. She promptly sits up and scoops him toward her with a gentle sweep of her great paw. He whines again, loud enough to wake his siblings. By the time they arrive, he is already chuckling away on his side of the food line. As the other cubs approach, he tries to straight-arm them away, even while still latched onto a nipple. He is boldly claiming all of his mother for himself. But she huffs at him, then scoops the others in for a meal.

With everyone on board, she nuzzles and sniffs each of them in turn. Carefully, she lies down on her back, wraps both forelegs around the huddle of nursing cubs and closes her eyes.

The cry of startled ravens wakes the mother bear. They sound more alarmed than angry, and there is a strong new scent in the air. She flips to her belly, dumping the sleeping cubs, and stands up on her hind legs. Slowly swinging her head from side to side, inhaling in deep, rapid sniffs, she determines that it is the scent of her own kind. Grizzly.

Sniff . . . It's a male . . . *sniff* . . . coming toward them along the blood trail. She peers in the direction of Excalibur Lake, but her view is broken by the rocks. The ravens flap away.

Sniff . . . Another scent . . . *Sniff* . . . *sniff.* The afternoon heat plays tricks with the wind, and this new ribbon of scent is in tatters before she can identify it. She drops down and growls a sharp command to her cubs. Still half asleep, they dawdle, and she barks again. They scramble to her side and sniff the stirred-up breeze for whatever upset their mother.

She stops sniffing. From behind the rocks, a yearling grizzly and his mother march boldly into view. Both are as blond as dried tundra grass.

The bear on the meat cache rears up halfway, then drops to all fours with a loud roar. The cubs peek around her sides to look at the visitors and add a few feeble growls of their own. With a couple of quick jabs of her rear legs she bowls them backward to safety.

The two adult bears glare at each other across the meat cache. Its rightful owner snaps her jaws, making hollow popping noises. Then, with a bellow, she breaks into a charge. She gallops full speed at the intruders. Between each bound she slashes the air with her orange claws. She bares her teeth and out of her throat comes a terrible descending growl that her shivering cubs have never heard.

The intruding female holds her ground just long enough for her cub to escape. Then she, too, bolts for the lake. The attacker roars her way through the maze of rocks and chases them clear out onto the ice before turning back.

Reclaiming her cache, she finds three ravens have beat her to it. She is still fired up from her chase and lunges at them, flashing her claws and bellowing as she did for the bears. The ravens vanish. The cubs emerge from under a knot of willow sticks, wailing for their mother.

Over the next two days, the big bear remains parked resolutely on top of her meat cache. Though her appetite is gradually returning, she eats little. She mostly sleeps, draped belly down over the rotting carcasses with her cubs finding what nest they can in her arms.

When would-be thieves arrive, she defends her cache with brute force and ferocity. Among the ousted visitors, drawn by the fetid odor of death, are two wolverines, a pack of five wolves, one golden eagle, and, surprisingly, that mother bear and yearling cub. Like everybody else, they are ruthlessly kicked out. Nothing and nobody can make this bear give up her claim.

But then she hears it. A steady whine, getting louder fast. There is no scent to warn her. No time to run. Without looking up she barks a command to her frolicking cubs and herds them swiftly toward the willows. She gathers them in close before crashing into the thickest shrubs. The prickly branches scratch the cubs' eyes and tender hides. Only when deep within the thicket, with her cubs in her arms, does she cock her head to the sky.

The noise increases, a rattling drone that seems to spill from the sun. Through the willows, she spots a huge shadow streaking toward their hiding place. It darts and rolls madly across the jumble of towering boulders. For a split second it blankets the bears, who cling tight with closed eyes.

Then . . . it's gone. The noise. The shadow. But not the fear. The big male cub tries to struggle free but his mother will not let go. She knows it might return and encourages them to nurse. Which they do. Until it does come back.

She spots it this time. An airplane. It wheels above them. Around it goes, in tighter and tighter circles until it seems to hang in the air spinning on one wing pointed at their heads.

In a rash act that threatens to give them away, the big bear drops the cubs from her arms and shakes her deadly foreclaws at the plane. It keeps circling, like a determined eagle fixed on a meal.

The bear hunkers down in defeat. The cubs bawl and hide their faces in their mother's fur. They scratch and dig at her chest as if trying to burrow inside.

When the plane finally flies away, the bear doesn't stir for several minutes. Every whine from her cubs is rewarded with a swift cuff. She knows she must listen and watch.

That rattling drone. It's coming back. She sees a flash of yellow. The plane swoops so low it almost touches the top of her cache.

They can have it as far as she's concerned. After another hour of hiding, she bursts out of the willows and heads for the rocky hills as fast as her whining cubs will let her.

"You should've worn your cowboy hat for that one, Siku," says Ozzie in the back seat of the Beaver.

"Boss's orders," says Siku. "Buzz the bear's cache."

"I can't believe we didn't see her," says Vicky.

Ozzie is tugging his beard. "Why do you need to see her *that* bad when we can track her with the satellite?"

"The satellite data from January suggests Triple Seven gave birth to three cubs."

"So what's the rush?"

"The first weeks out of the den are the most dangerous for cubs. We have to get to them now while they're all still alive."

"Cubs die, Vicky."

"Of course, but if the satellite says she had three cubs, and we actually *see* three cubs, we'll add further proof to the incredible value of this technology."

"And maybe convince Gloss to buy you more of those expensive collars?"

"Exactly. He keeps threatening to pull the plug on us."

"Do you honestly think your fancy data will impress him? All he cares about grizzlies is that they don't eat his high-paid staff."

"Then how *should* we impress him?"

"There's always Benji."

"Who?"

"Gloss's kid. Get him fired up over grizzlies, and it's bound to rub off on his dad."

"He's too citified. Besides, I think Buster spooked him when he charged the chopper."

"Can't hurt. I got an e-mail from Benji yesterday," Ozzie laughs. "He addressed it, 'Dear Scat-man.' Says he's coming up in mid-June."

"He'll only get in our way."

"His dad'll dump him on us anyway, so we might as well show him a good time."

"Charm him up, you mean?"

"We won't have to do the charming. The bears will do that for us. Call it Project Benji."

EARLY
SUMMER

CHAPTER 7

FREE FALL

The bond between a mother bear and her cubs is greatest in the
    first spring and summer of the cubs' lives.
—*Wayne Lynch*, Bears

June 15. Benji's attic room, San Francisco.

"So what's the big attraction up north?" asks Brad as he idly surfs
through the hundreds of channels on Benji's mega TV. "I thought
you called it a wasteland."

Benji stuffs CDs into an old suitcase he always takes on mine
tours. "It's sure not the food." He tosses in a handful of chocolate
bars. "Emergency rations. In case our chopper goes down."

"They let you fly it?"

"Not yet."

"I thought your dad ran the show. Couldn't he just order the
pilot to hand over the joystick?"

"He never comes. I think he's allergic to choppers."

"Or grizzlies maybe?"

Benji laughs. "Yeah, maybe."

The world's fastest creature streaks out of the gray arctic sky. A female peregrine falcon aims squarely at the big bear's head. The bear family, marching along a high cliff above Fortune Creek, is too close to her nest. Just before impact she thrusts out her wings and extends her razor-sharp talons.

A sound like knife edges slashing the air makes the mother bear tilt her nose skyward. This one small gesture presents the angry bird with the most vulnerable of targets.

In the blink of an eye, her talons stab deep wounds into the bear's muzzle. The blow sends her sprawling in pain, almost trampling the cubs, who instinctively run for cover beneath her collapsing legs. She lands on her back in a rocky bed of Labrador tea. The whining cubs, familiar with this inviting pose, climb on board for a reassuring suckle—which their mother is in no mood for. After cuffing them aside, she cradles her wounded nose between her forepaws, casting guarded glances into an empty sky.

The cubs whine and fuss. Their mother moans. Her muzzle drips blood. She rolls onto her stomach and shoves it into a pool of meltwater, which soon turns red. The cubs watch their mother blow bubbles. A nursing session is long overdue.

With a sudden squeal, the runt male jumps on her back and starts digging through her fur like a dog looking for a lost bone. The female cub scampers up to her mother's head and tugs her ear. The big male cub sits on his haunches waiting for something to happen. Nothing. Just more bloody bubbles. His mother is preoccupied with pain.

The big male blows a fuse. He bolts upright, looking for something to attack. He needs a punching bag for his raging frustration.

His chosen victim: a small hummock of Labrador tea topped with cottongrass. The little bear charges the hummock, exactly as he'd seen his mother charge those nosey bears at the meat cache . . . sort of. To a flea or maybe a mouse his charge would be terrifying. Between fumbling leaps, he slashes the air with his baby claws. He squeaks savagely at the innocent plants. He pounces belly down on the hummock and wrestles it into submission. For good measure, he rips out all the cottongrass with his bared fangs.

The female cub is captivated. She makes a surprise attack from the rear, knocking her big brother flat. Before he's up, she dashes away, then springs to a wobbly stand, just begging for a counterattack, which he gladly provides. This battle goes on until the big male, while lunging for his sister, fumbles and sails over the edge of the cliff.

The female cub runs bawling to her mother, who is still soaking her wounds. Out of habit, she jumps smack onto her mother's nose, which certainly gets her attention. Her mother lurches to her feet. The runt male, who'd been asleep on her back, wakes with a start. He manages to hang on by gripping her satellite collar, a trick he's learned from his big brother.

The big bear instantly knows something's wrong. She bats the female cub out of the way, trots over to a hump of bedrock and springs to a stand. The runt male, though squealing up a storm, remains solidly clamped to her collar while his hind legs dangle freely in the air. His mother peers all around, woofing loudly for the big male.

She sniffs hard, discovering not the soothing scent of her lost cub but a searing pain that claws through her muzzle to the crown of her skull. She tries another deep sniff but only flinches. The turpentine smell of Labrador tea flowers is all that filters through the fire in her nose. The falcon's talons have robbed her of the master key that unlocks the signs and secrets of her world.

The north wind stiffens, obliterating even the strongest scents. Cottongrass and dwarf birch lean away from the wind as if trying to escape. The bear cautiously looks up. She spots two black specks dropping from the clouds and fixes them in her gaze. If those are peregrine falcons, she won't be caught off guard this time.

The specks turn into black smudges—ravens, diving straight at her. They boldly drop almost to within striking distance, then pull up into an unflapping hover. They cock their heads, inspecting the huddle of bears with short, jerky stares. Slight twists of their tails keep them glued to one spot as the wind rushes past. It's as if they, too, are looking for the lost cub, hoping to pick it apart.

A surge in the wind lifts the ravens high above the bears. They drop down near the cliff edge. They sway and somersault in the fountains of wind gushing up from below. Then something catches their eyes, and they plummet out of sight.

In spite of her crippled nose, the mother bear needs no more clues to figure out what happened to her missing cub. The ravens are on to him. She drops to all fours and runs toward the cliff, abruptly halting a paw's length from the edge. The runt male, still on her back, keeps going and flips backward onto her head. Were it not for his firm grip on her collar, he, too, would have sailed off into thin air.

The big bear rolls back on her haunches, swats the whimpering cub off her back, then rolls forward to look over the edge. The top of the cliff sticks out in great bedrock humps like elephant bums. A tiny moss-covered ledge sticks out below. Farther down is a jagged field of bear-sized boulders.

Without that ledge, the big male cub would be raven snack. But the instant the mother bear sticks her head over the side, she's greeted with his familiar bawling. The cub appears uninjured as he jumps and claws at the rocks far below. But there seems no safe escape route off the ledge. Meanwhile the ravens float above the marooned cub, playing tag on the wing while waiting for it to die.

The falcon chooses this moment to strike again. The cub is about to scramble her eggs, which lie on the ledge near his hopping paws. She takes aim at the mother crouched on the cliff edge with her head still over the side.

The bear catches that slashing noise again just in time. In a flash, she covers her eyes and wounded nose and braces her shoulders for the impact. It comes a split second later, not as a piercing, tearing blow but a dull thud, as if she's been struck on the neck by a falling branch. The falcon hit the collar, her talons carving a deep gash through the leather.

While her two cubs huddle close, the big bear holds her pose. Again the bird dive-bombs the collar, mistaking it for a tender patch of exposed bearskin. Four attacks, four slashes at the collar. Only after the bear hears the falcon's *ki-ki-ki-ki* alarm call does she dare look up. The bird flies high above them in wide, broken circles. After a final, menacing dive, she vanishes.

The ravens, who kept a safe distance during the attacks, now hover ominously close to the stranded cub.

All three bears stand up on their hind legs, looking for the phantom falcon. The mother bear growls at the clouds, then walks away.

For fourteen springs she has visited this cliff and knows well the best way down. She grunts at her two remaining cubs, then clambers down a mossy chute that slopes safely through the elephant-shaped rocks.

At the bottom of the cliff, the chute spills out into the boulder field. Rotten snow still hugs the shadowed base of the cliff. These feed invisible streams that gurgle noisily below the boulders. The cubs cling to her and soon are riding on her back like camel drivers.

Except for a few crusty lichens, the boulder field is as lifeless as the moon. But right below the ledge with the stranded cub is a clump of willows much taller than a standing grizzly. Thick moss and grasses flourish around their trunks.

The big bear makes straight for the willows. Few smells get through the pain in her nose. But she can plainly see what's going on here.

Littering the lush moss are the sun-bleached bones of countless ducks, sparrows, and ground squirrels. The bear looks up the rock wall. It's smeared with bird droppings so white it almost glows. For hundreds, maybe thousands of years, generations of falcons have used this perch as a nest site, hunting platform, and toilet bowl. Their dregs and debris, trickling down the rocks, created this island of life in an otherwise barren moonscape.

What spills over the edge now is not bones or droppings but the desperate wail of one lost cub. To the amusement of the other two, their mother grabs the tallest willows and starts thrashing them with all her might. One breaks off. She goes at them with less punch, twiddling the tallest one with her paw while looking up the rock face and woofing loudly.

The top of the shaken willow reaches almost to the stranded cub's ledge. Its lime green leaves wave back and forth in front of his nose. He doesn't get it. Seeing his mother down there, so close yet so far, only adds to his misery, so he sits there, bawling to the sky.

His mother shakes the willow more violently, risking destruction of the cub's only escape route. She erupts with three thunderous bellows delivered in scolding tones. The two cubs at her feet mimic her calls with a few squeaky barks.

One of the ravens dares to land near the lone cub, who, out of habit, tries to smack it. Now feeling more playful, he looks again at the strangely waving willows in front of him. He lies down on his belly and, like a cat toying with a ball of yarn, leans out to swat the glistening leaves. His mother pushes the willow closer to him. He leans out farther, still swatting. She bellows again and again, her awesome roars echoing off the big boulders all around her.

Suddenly, the big male cub is again in flight, this time crashing down through the branches of the tall willow. As his mother had hoped, the branches break his fall. He tumbles, head over claws, from one branch to another, then bounces off her back. He lands with a thump and a grunt on top of his siblings. They welcome him back to earth with swift whacks to his head and nips to his ears.

CHAPTER 8

FISHING HOLE

To him almost everything is food except granite.
—*John Muir*, Bears

June 18.

"More holidays with your dad?" Siku asks Benji, whose father just sped back to the mining camp in a truck.

Benji has mixed feelings about being back here—about his bear-hugging baby-sitters, about the chance to see a grizzly up close, even about more helicopter joyrides. "Holidays? That's what *he* calls them."

"Why doesn't he join us?"

"Too busy. Too chicken. How should I know?" Benji notices Siku slipping on a pair of black, skintight flying gloves with little holes at the knuckles. "What's with the designer gloves?"

"They help me feel if anything's falling apart."

Benji strokes the helicopter's gleaming black skin. "Not *this* machine. It's built solid."

"You never know, kid. Climb in. I'll show you how to fly this thing in case I croak up there."

Benji straightens up. "What?"

"Fifteen-minute flight lesson."

He can't believe his ears. After building model helicopters since he was in diapers, after subscribing to *Heliventure* magazine since he could read, after riding in helicopters at mines all over the world, no one has let him actually *fly* one.

Then he remembers: the fear that gripped his insides when he first glimpsed the empty barren-lands from the air. That feeling of being a gutless speck of nothing. Of all the places his father had taken Benji—the Arizona desert, the Peruvian mountains, the jungles of New Guinea—no landscape had ever made him feel so small, so worthless.

The machine's wasplike tail catches his eye. Benji's love of helicopters runs deep. It must have been something I ate, he figures, sweeping the dark memory aside.

"Were flight lessons my dad's idea?"

"Vicky's actually."

"But somebody's paying for . . ."

"Yep. Seven hundred bucks an hour. Vicky called it . . . an investment." Siku shrugs. "Something about . . . Project Benji. Hop in, kid. Front seat."

The big bear's wounds heal rapidly. Already, the dark scabs on her nose have begun to split and fall off, revealing tender, new skin beneath. But she can't cut and peel the air the way she could before the falcon attack. Most of the fresh sweet scents of green-up are entirely lost to her injured nose. Those talons dug deep and even the smallest sniff still sends a hot, stabbing pain to much of her head.

Handicapped as she is, she can still detect a thick dampness in the air. Compared to the boulder-strewn meadows of much of her domain, the Fortune Creek valley is an oasis. Its rich soils produce a bumper crop of horsetails, grasses, and tundra flowers. In the wetter spots, sedge tussocks form what look like herds of sleeping porcupines with quills swept back by the wind. Lush willows line the creek, providing shelter from the midday heat for a pile of sleeping bears.

The bears wake to the chatter of redpolls: *chet-chet-chet, boing, boing, chet-chet-chet.* The cubs are hungry, as they always are when they wake. Their food supply is as handy as ever. Their mother's is not. As the cubs suckle on her warm belly, it grumbles below them for lack of nourishment. These days her belly is usually full, sometimes painfully so. But in early summer, even as the land gushes green, quality food for a tundra grizzly is in short supply.

On her menu are wiry horsetails and sedges, sour willow leaves, and flimsy arctic flowers. She'll eat the shrunken fruits from last fall's berry crop. She'll pounce on a shrew or lemming. Or she'll spend an afternoon digging up half a hillside for one small squirrel. Sometimes she'll even hunt down stinging wasps and ants. Despite stuffing herself with these tundra tidbits, she steadily loses weight.

The haunting shadow of hunger drives the mother bear out of her comfortable daybed and toward the creek. Her well-fed cubs watch closely as she yanks out a clump of sedges by the roots and stuffs it into her mouth, dirt and all. The big male tries to imitate his mother but gets no further than wrestling with some sedges that won't let go. While the other two cubs join forces in the attack, their mother slips into the creek and waddles downstream.

The cubs trip along the tangled creek bank, doing their best to keep up. They have never seen so much water, let alone swam in it.

The big bear wades fearlessly into deeper, faster waters as the creek becomes choked between two fists of bedrock. Here it froths and foams, gathering enough power to carry a small cub to its doom.

Up to her neck in rushing water, the big bear stops at the narrows to examine a large walrus-shaped boulder breaking the surface. For the moment, she ignores the cubs, whose whines are smothered by the water's roar. She climbs carefully onto the slippery back of the walrus—like a circus seal balancing on a ball—and starts swiping her forepaw across its downstream side. Unable to see through the froth, she knows what's down there. A hard-up hunger has driven her to this rock before.

After each swipe, the bear takes a close look at her paw. Swipe, look. Swipe, look. There . . . standing out against an orange claw: something black, something squirming. She aims her long tongue at the tiny wormlike target, then swipes again. Three more. Lick, lick, lick. Now she plunges her head into the swirling water, feeling for the boulder's base. This time she lifts a paw covered in black glistening slime. Yum. A writhing mass of blackfly larvae. She licks her paw clean. Another few swipes and the boulder is bare. This puny appetizer of insect protein only fuels her gnawing hunger.

"How was your driving lesson?" asks Ozzie as Siku lifts off for a second time this morning.

"Awesome," says Benji, now in the back seat. "That joystick sure is touchy."

"That was a crash course, kid" says Siku. "Just another hundred hours to get your license."

Benji's thoughts are pulled from the morning's treat of flying to the vast landscape now sprawling out below. Too distracted by Siku's instructions, or perhaps too scared, he barely looked at it earlier. He leans hesitantly into the bubble window and looks down.

Everything's changed since mid-May. The tundra's oceanlike scale still makes him shudder. Maybe his friend, Brad, was right about being afraid of open spaces. But somehow the land seems less forbidding, less empty. Like the back of a giant chameleon, the tundra has changed all its colors, trading white, brown, and gray for a fresh fuzz of lime and emerald greens. Most ponds and lakes are ice free, reflecting the sky's darkest shades of blue. Benji soon can't keep his eyes off the scene. Then the chatter starts up again in his headset.

"Where to, boss?" says Siku.

"Fortune Creek," says Vicky. "The satellite says Triple Seven's been hanging around there for several days. Either her collar's fallen off, or she's found a good food source."

"Or she's dead," says Siku.

"She's only fourteen, Siku. She was fit as a fiddle when we darted her last August on top of Excalibur esker. Remember? Blueberries everywhere."

"Roger." Siku tips the joystick forward, then calls down to camp. "Yankee Echo Bravo to Saber. Do you copy?"

"Saber here."

"We'll be heading twelve miles northeast to Fortune Creek. We'll probably put down there to collect bear turds and have lunch."

"In what order?" asks the Saber voice.

Then Benji hears Saber's channel suddenly go dead. He gives Ozzie a puzzled look.

"You're not supposed to laugh over official flight channels," he explains.

"I'll keep you posted on that," says Siku.

Saber clicks back on. "The drill crew spotted a mean-looking bear down there yesterday as they flew back to camp."

Vicky cuts in. "Were any cubs spotted?"

"No cubs, Vic. The boys said the bear ran out in the open when they flew by. It stood up, staring at 'em. Looked mean."

"Did it have a collar?"

"Couldn't see. The boys said you told them not to fly low over your bears."

"Any distinguishing features?"

"They just said it was big and ugly."

"It's probably Triple Seven."

"Who?"

"Triple Seven. That's her collar number."

"Right. Good hunting, folks. Saber Camp clear."

"That's strange," says Vicky. "I've never known her to stand up to any aircraft. Usually she runs like hell."

Siku says nothing. He's paid to fly, not figure out which bears are doing what, why, and when. That's her job.

The mother bear glances over at her cubs on the creek bank. The big male reaches out into the current as far as he can, bravely batting a restless wave. His siblings, crouched behind him, chew nervously on each other's faces. Their mother woofs, then moves downstream.

Farther on, she climbs onto a granite slab sticking high and dry out of the water. The creek still runs fast here, but behind the rock is a large eddy of smooth water into which she looks with hungry interest.

If she can't sniff out a decent meal, she can at least use her eyes to watch for a tasty fish. She knows the fishing is good here. It's only a matter of time. Usually.

The creek widens at this point, and the cubs are too far away for her liking. There's lots of room on this rock. It's a safe, dry haven for the whole family. Coaxing them to swim out to her would be disastrous. She takes another quick look into the eddy—no fish—then plunges into the powerful current.

She emerges streamside, looking like a giant, underfed dog, and shakes all over the cubs. Water spirals off the ruff of her neck, which looks like a clown's collar. Two of the cubs climb all over her. In this case, it is exactly what she wants. The big male is first on her back and latches onto her satellite collar. In turn, the female cub clamps both forelegs around his waist. The ferrying begins. With her two riders locked on board, the mother bear dives back in.

The rush of water all around the big male is almost too exciting. He unlatches one paw and starts batting waves again like a playful cat. His sister clings to his haunches as she rides out the great heaves and rolls of her mother's back. Left alone on the creek bank, the runt male bawls loudly enough to be heard even above the clamor of water.

Before the mother bear gets a paw up on the dry slab, the big male rockets off her back, towing his sister with him through the air. He lands on the rock. She doesn't. Still latched to her brother, her hindquarters flop helplessly in the white water tearing past the rock. But her grip is sure, and the big male unwittingly saves her life as he bounds forward to explore this tiny new territory.

By the time the mother bear returns to the runt, he is beside himself with glee. He jumps onto her head and tumbles off. He squeezes under her wet belly trying to nurse. He wraps himself around a leg, but she flings him off with a quick shake. He doesn't understand that his only ticket across is to climb on her back.

His mother ignores him for a while, chowing down clumps of horsetails and fireweed buds. Then she turns tail and gallops into the water. Halfway across she halts abruptly and looks back at her bawling cub. She returns, he licks her nose, and she jumps in again. This goes on four times before he finally gets the message and climbs onto her back. In the excitement, he forgets about the collar trick and struggles to get a good grip on her thick, wet fur.

This time, instead of waddling across, his mother leaps forward, two paws at a time. This is too much for the runt and he slips over her starboard, upstream side. On his way, he manages to clench a mouthful of fur before his head goes under. Any bawling at this point would mean the end of him. Luckily, he keeps his mouth shut and the great pressure of water bearing down on them keeps him glued to her side. After thrashing about, he's able to get one hind leg up on her back, then hook a foreleg under her collar. Clinging to a wet wall of fur, he rides the rest of the way sidesaddle through the waves. His mother dumps him on the rock, where he is pounced on by his siblings.

After a spell of nursing and a family nap, the mother bear settles down to the business of fishing.

First, she lies belly down on the eddy side of the rock with her chin propped on a paw. She looks intently into the smooth water. For a long time she doesn't move a muscle. The cubs fuss behind her, but she silences them with a grunt. She sticks in her other forepaw and idly paddles the slowly churning water. After a while, she sticks her head in and swings it back and forth. Her ears resemble twin periscopes just breaking the surface. She does this for a long time, blowing bubbles that the big male swats with his paw.

Finally, she pulls herself back from the water's edge and again falls asleep in spite of the chronic hunger burning in her belly.

When she wakes, it's back to snorkeling. Of course, all the cubs have to try this, and for a while the fishing rock is rimmed on one side with four bubbling bears. Later the cubs put their paws in, swinging at who knows what. None of them has seen a fish before, but their mother's lessons have never led them astray. Their teacher soon realizes that there's way too much commotion for any serious fishing, and she shoos them away.

By now the sun has swung round enough to send dark blue shadows across most of the bear's fishing hole. The midday glare on the water is gone, and she can see clearly from one end of the eddy to the other. There *are* fish down there. She spots at least four arctic grayling at the far end of the pool. They all face upstream, their long, lacy fins quivering slightly.

"There she is," says Siku.

"The bear?" asks Vicky, lunging forward to the limits of her seat belt.

"The creek." Siku pulls back on the joystick, putting on the brakes about a mile back from Fortune Creek.

"What's up?" asks Benji.

"This isn't a darting exercise," says Ozzie. "No need to spook Triple Seven if we don't have to."

"Very good, Siku," says Vicky. "Hold her steady here for a minute." From under her seat Vicky pulls out a leather-covered box about the size of a toaster. Benji can see all kinds of animals embossed on the leather—elk, mountain sheep, cougars, grizzlies. With growing interest, he leans forward and watches Vicky unsnap the top of the box to reveal a control panel bristling with silver switches. She flicks three and the numbers 7–7–7 appear on a small screen. Then she plugs a wire into the helicopter dash, and a stream of electronic beeps floods his ears.

"Can you turn that thing down?" says Benji. "Whatever it is."

"Telemetry box," explains Ozzie. "Vicky's favorite toy. Those beeps are music to her ears."

"Is that like telepathy? Reading a bear's thoughts?"

Ozzie laughs. "The technology's not quite there, Benji. But you can be sure Vicky'll be first in line when it is."

"Nothing saying they can't read *our* thoughts," says Siku.

"Kill the chatter, guys," says Vicky. "I need to concentrate on her signal. We'll find her this time. We have to."

Boy! thinks Benji. What's *she* so obsessed about? It's just a bear. But even as he thinks this, his eyes unconsciously sweep the valley for the phantom grizzly. With Triple Seven's beeps ringing in his headset, his searching gaze runs from a high cliff along one side, to a field of boulders, some green meadows, and finally to a tangle of thick willows lining Fortune Creek.

As they fly closer to the boulder field, Benji suddenly feels queasy. It's like he's been here before. A dim memory of slipping. Falling. Running for a cave. With a she-bear on his heels.

Without taking her eyes off the fish, the mother bear inches a foreleg into the water. Her long orange claws dangle near the pebbly bottom of the pool, waving loosely in the subtle currents. The fish slowly back away.

A shaft of sunlight catches the side of one fish. It flashes iridescent blues and greens into the bear's brown eyes. Saliva seeps into the corners of her mouth. Her stomach rumbles.

She lures the fish with her fearsome claws. They stop, pause, then, moving as one, advance toward them. Something in the claws' color or gentle motion draws the fish closer, closer. The bear's body is relaxed, her awareness totally concentrated. Soon the boldest fish, takes a nip at a claw. The others form a line behind as if waiting for their turn.

The bear's foreleg stiffens slightly, her claws twitch. As a second grayling moves in for a nip, the first makes the final tail-flick of its life, placing it exactly where the bear wants it—between her claws and the jagged base of the rock. *Slam!* The fish is thrust against the rock, then expertly scooped out of the water. *Whack!* The bear smashes the fish against the dry slab right under the noses of her startled cubs.

It's a big grayling, well over two pounds, but really not much for a full grown grizzly. She rips off the head and gills and chews them with noisy relish. Then the skin, fins and all, is stripped and eaten. Finally she teases the guts from the carcass and downs the flesh and eggs in several quick gulps. The cubs probe the fish guts with their noses, then leave them for the scavengers. Already, just seconds after the first catch, four gulls circle overhead.

She looks back into the pool. The remaining fish stay in the eddy swimming in wide circles as if trapped. The bear cocks her right forepaw high in the air. Slowly, she leans forward over the water keeping her paw ready to strike. Her head spins slightly with the twirling fish. She chooses the slowest fish. Here it comes, swimming around. It's right below her. *Slam!* In an explosion of spray, her lightning paw comes down and pins the fish against the rock. She scoops it out and eats it exactly like the first. The other grayling escape into the ring of white water, but soon more fish enter the still pool and circle around.

The big bear's timing is good. Since she was first brought to this rock by her mother fourteen summers ago, she has always arrived at the peak of the spawning run. Soon her fishing rock will be smeared with the red residue of grayling.

Hovering high above Fortune Creek valley, Siku turns to Vicky. "What's the plan, boss?"

"I'm sure Triple Seven's somewhere along the creek. I want a low sweep down its length. Comb the willows. Start from that snow-patch up there, and fly right down to Lost Lake. That should flush her out. You got that, Siku?"

"Whatever."

Let the bear hunt begin, thinks Benji, tightening his seat belt.

Four gulls circle above the fishing bear. The cubs boldly swing at them when they try to steal any morsels. A male bald eagle, not intimidated by clumsy cubs, scatters the gulls in a flurry of white feathers. Without braking, he deftly extends his blazing yellow talons and snatches a gut pile off the fishing rock. His victory is short-lived. Right behind him is a larger female eagle who harasses him with broadside lunges until he drops his bloody prize. She plucks the spinning entrails from the air. The big bear stares into the pool, not once looking up at the battles right above her head.

The cubs have enjoyed the air show and stand in a row on their hind legs. Now they bob their noses, detecting a new scent in the dying breezes. Above the rank odor of fish, there's something heavy and alien in the air. The smell makes them drop to all fours and run for their mother. The female cub climbs on her back and clamps on. The runt curls into a trembling ball at her feet. The big male's fear is eclipsed by his curiosity. He jumps to his hind feet, sniffing hard.

Surely his mother would know what it is. He yanks on his mother's collar. She ignores him. He chews on her ear. She swats him off like a pesky bug and continues staring intently into the water. As strange as this new scent is, her wounded nose fails her and she misses it completely.

A flock of ptarmigan erupts from the willows downstream. The mother bear finally looks up. Hearing nothing but white water, smelling nothing much at all, she has only her eyes to weigh the approaching danger. She squints into the willows. The tallest ones sway madly. Whatever spooked those ptarmigan is headed straight for the blood-soaked fishing rock.

There is no time to coax the runt onto her back. She picks him up by the scruff of his neck and crashes into the creek. The big male clamps onto her collar while looking at the crazy commotion behind them. The female cub clenches her eyes under the blows of her bucking brother. Just as they emerge from the rushing water, a huge male grizzly bear crashes out of the willows on the opposite bank.

CHAPTER 9

CRACK-UP

Of every two grizzly cubs born, one will die in the first eighteen
  months. Male bears or unrelated females are the main killers.
  For many cubs, life is short and brutish.
—*Grizzly*

That's perfect, Siku," says Vicky as he lines up the helicopter over
the snow-patch feeding Fortune Creek. "Nice and slow. When
the willows get thick, I want you to zigzag from one bank to the
other so we can peek right in. Triple Seven's not getting away
from us this time."

The beeps in Benji's headset get louder and louder. He figures
this must be a happy sound for a bear biologist. He's never seen
Vicky in such a good mood. She leans far forward, her head sweeping back and forth as if she were humming a jolly tune. Her fingers
do a lively dance against the telemetry box on her lap. She's actually smiling. This goes on until Benji sees Siku's black-gloved finger
point to the fuel gauge, then spread his hand five fingers wide.

Vicky's head jolts backward. "Only five minutes?"

"Bit of a problem, boss," says Siku. "My reserve tank won't kick
in for some reason. That cuts our fuel supply in half."

"Five minutes will barely get us halfway down the creek!"

"Safety first. Bears second," says Siku.

"But you've got almost a quarter tank left."

"I'll give you eight minutes max. Then it's home sweet home, ma'am, bears or no bears."

Vicky pinches her lower lip with her fingers. "Okay, then. Go straight down the creek."

The two bears glare at each other from opposite sides of the creek. She has seen him before but never so close. The sight triggers a prickling in her scalp. He's a giant, almost twice her size. His matted fur is the color of wet peat. His massive head is almost perfectly round. She springs to her hind feet to get a better look. Half an ear is missing, along with several of his dark orange foreclaws. A gaping scar slants between his eyes and down his muzzle. Two fresh wounds on his shoulder appear to be draining yellow pus.

The intruder rears up to his full stature and jerks his great head from side to side. He lets out a deafening bellow aimed squarely at the mother bear. He drops into the shallows with an enormous splash, but makes only a couple of bluff charges as if hesitant to plunge right in. Then, in one colossal stride, he leaps from bank to fishing rock. For a moment he ignores the she-bear and her cubs as he gulps down piles of fish guts and clotted blood.

The mother bear does not hang around to see what he'll do next. She plows into the willows still carrying the whining, kicking runt in her mouth. The female cub hunkers down on her back with eyes still closed. Her big brother sits on top of her, riding bronco-style but in reverse. He wants to get a good look at the huge bear now bounding toward them across the last stretch of rapids.

A thick willow branch suddenly clips the male cub in the head, spilling him onto a patch of moss. For a moment he is alone, torn between fear and curiosity. He wants one more good whiff of the strange beast advancing toward him. A cool waft of air from the creek fills his nostrils with a musky sourness. His button nose crinkles. He risks a final sniff, to imprint this alarming scent forever in his brain, then scrambles after his mother.

The beeps ringing in Benji's ears are so loud he can't tell if they are swelling or fading in volume.

"We've got her this time," says Vicky. "She must be right below us."

At a sharp narrowing of the creek, where the water flows white, Benji spots a blue fin breaking the foamy surface. "Salmon?"

"Grayling," says Ozzie.

Just downstream Benji sees a large rock slab in the middle of the current with a smooth pool behind it. He squints at the rock. "What the . . . ?" It's coated with red slime.

Ozzie sees it, too, "That's gotta be blood. Look! It's covered in grizzly tracks."

Just as the male cub breaks out of the willows onto a wet meadow, he hears deep coughing noises right behind him. The giant's hot breath almost scorches his heels. Running full speed toward the cub from the opposite direction is his mother. She bravely charges the intruder with flashing claws and thunderous roars. But she is no match for this brute and suddenly veers off at the last moment just a hair from her squealing cub. The cub veers, too, but not quickly enough. His little paws stick in the muck.

The mother bear watches helplessly as the giant grizzly clamps down on her cub's bobbing rump. He grabs the cub, flings it into the air like a mouse, then gives it a few twisting shakes that end with a hollow snap. Then, with the limp cub hanging from his jaws, he plunges back into the willows and heads for the creek.

Into the terror of this scene comes a new sound that stirs memories of panic stored deep in the mother bear's brain. A choking blanket of sound slides above the desperate whining of her two remaining cubs and the white noise of the hidden creek. Swiftly it comes, a low, pounding, insect noise.

"There she is!" yells Vicky, pointing to the left bank.

Benji looks over just in time to see a dark brown shape disappear into the willows.

Ozzie is shaking his head. "That's no mama bear," he says. "Not Triple Seven at least."

"What?" says Vicky.

"That's not her," he says. "Too big. Too dark."

"And no collar," adds Benji, who had the best view of the fleeing bear.

"Mighta been Buster," says Ozzie.

"No way. He's long gone," says Vicky as she sticks two thumbs up. Siku circles a few times over the willows. Vicky points to the wet meadow beyond. "Must have scared it off. Let's put down there. I want to look for cub tracks."

Siku does one low sweep over the meadow, then pulls back on his joystick.

"What are you doing?" asks Vicky. "I thought you could land anywhere with these floats."

"Not in this mush."

"How about that slimy rock back there?" says Benji. "The red one."

Ozzie nods. "Fresh tracks all over it."

"It's big enough," says Siku. "We could do it. As long as you clean the blood off my floats."

With the skill of a dragonfly landing on a lily pad, Siku gently lowers his chopper onto the rock slab. A fine mist of blood coats Benji's window as they land. "I think I messed up your tracks," says Siku as he powers down.

"Not all of them." Vicky points to some crusty red tracks beside the eddy. "Cub for sure. That clinches it. Triple Seven *is* a mom. You got any hip waders, Siku? We could cross the creek and look for . . ."

Ozzie suddenly cuts in. "That's no cub!"

Through a veil of blood, Benji sees Buster charge out of the willows. "Whoa!" The bear is so close, Benji can see that one of his claws is missing. Those claws . . . he can't look at them. There's something dark dangling from his jaws. "What's in his mouth?"

"It's Vicky's cub," says Ozzie. "Chewed up pretty bad. Let's scram, Siku!"

Siku throttles up to full power as Vicky dodges around him with her camera. "We've got to document this on film. . . . Look! Half his ear is gone! And check out those scars!"

Above the pounding of the helicopter's rotors, Benji feels the hammering of his heart. Just feet away stands a battle-scarred beast chomping on one of its own kind. "How could he *do* that?"

"It's a bear-eat-bear world out there, Benji," says Ozzie. "Adult males aren't big on family. That might even be his own cub."

A swirling mix of disgust and horror floods Benji's thoughts. At the sight of this beast, so raw and savage, he feels stripped of his own skin, revealing nothing inside but a hollow core of panic.

Siku hits a switch on the ceiling and blasts Buster with a police siren. The bear drops the cub, stands to his full height, and brandishes his yellow teeth.

"He hates helicopters, right?" asks Benji in a trembly voice. "He won't come nearer?"

Benji gets his answer just as one orange float lifts free from the rock. Buster charges.

"Boot it, Siku!" yells Ozzie.

The second float lifts off. A swirling spray of mist and blood envelopes the helicopter. Benji watches Buster gallop through the white water as if it were dry grass. Like a mad ballet star, he leaps onto the rock and springs to a stand in one smooth arc.

"He's right below us!" yells Benji.

"He's on your side, Benji," says Ozzie. "What's he doing?"

Benji has to press his nose against the window to see him. He pulls back suddenly when he sees dark orange claws thrashing the air just below the left float.

"He's going for your floats!"

"Hard right rudder, Siku!" yells Ozzie.

Siku struggles to go up and sideways at the same time.

"Watch the willows!" yells Vicky.

"Higher, Siku!" yells Ozzie.

Siku manages a quick sideslip but loses precious height. The left float falls within range of the grizzly's claws. There's another sideways lurch, this one executed by Buster.

Benji can't believe his eyes. He clamps them shut. His head floods with the image of stone claws far more terrible than Buster's. Benji is falling backward, screaming. His mother's frightened face appears. She reaches for him through a window. . . .

His eyes snap open at the sound of Siku's siren.

"Back off, Buster!" yells Siku.

An electronic alarm goes off. Benji sees a red light flashing on Siku's dash: CHECK ENGINE.

Vicky sees it, too. "Please, not here, Siku. Not now!"

"We're losing power!" yells Siku.

Benji glances at Siku. A ragged toothpick flies back and forth across his mouth in a blur.

"What the hell's going on down there, Benji?" yells Ozzie.

"Can't see him," Benji yells. "Is he on your side?"

"My window's too smeared with blood," says Vicky.

Siku stares blankly at his instrument gauges. Benji notices that most of them are red-lining.

Then Benji remembers the fish-eye mirror Siku told him about during his so-called flight lesson. It sticks out near the pilot's feet letting him see anything below the chopper. "Siku, check your fish-eye!"

Siku gives his head a quick shake. "Right." After glancing in the mirror, he utters a sound that Benji figures must be an Inuktitut swear word.

Benji loosens his seat belt and cranes forward. In the curved mirror he sees the distorted reflection of a huge grizzly bear hauling down on the strut between both floats. The hurricane wind from the rotor throws a ghostly halo of fine mist off the wet bear's back. "Holy . . ."

"What the hell's going on?" yells Vicky as the helicopter lurches downward.

"Illegal passenger," says Siku. "I'm gonna try to dump him in the hole. Time to go fishing, Buster." He eases the helicopter not up but forward.

Benji sees the bear hang on even as its hind legs drag across the bloody rock. Just before reaching the downstream edge of the rock, Siku jerks the helicopter up and, for a moment, the bear's rear claws leave the ground.

"He's flying!" yells Benji.

"Dump him!" yells Ozzie.

Siku gives him another well-timed siren blast. The bear lets go and does a belly flop into the fishing hole.

"Bull's-eye!" yells Siku after a rare belly laugh. He lifts the helicopter a hundred feet above the creek, then hovers for a moment.

Everyone looks down at the huge grizzly climbing out of the water. It shakes itself off, then raises one defiant forepaw at the helicopter. Ozzie laughs out loud. "I'd swear he's shaking his fist at us."

Benji laughs, too, though it feels more like crying.

"What's the damage report?" asks Siku.

Benji sees shreds of orange rubber flapping in the rotor wash. "Buster toasted your left float." Then he remembers an article he read in *Heliventure* magazine. A helicopter with a popped float tried to land on an angle. Its long rotor blades smashed into the ground. The machine flipped. Four people went up in smoke. "How you gonna land without chewing up your blades?"

"Good point, kid," says Siku. "I was just thinking that my . . ."

Another electronic alarm goes off, this time flashing the words *low fuel*.

Siku turns to Vicky. "That fancy dancing back there almost sucked us dry."

"Can we make it back to camp?"

"Maybe. The trouble will be landing."

Siku patches into the camp radio. "This is Yankee Echo Bravo to Saber mine. Do you copy?"

"Go ahead, YEB."

"We're just above Fortune Creek, headed back to camp."

"Catch any bears?"

"Negative. In fact, one caught us. Clawed up our left float. She's flat as a pancake."

"Anybody hurt?"

"Negative—and I want to keep it that way. I need you to knock over a couple fuel drums and secure them to the helipad so I can land my left side on them. That should bring us down level."

"Roger. Two drums sideways on the pad."

"Step on it, guys. We're running low on juice."

"Got it, Siku. Saber clear."

Siku takes the helicopter up another couple hundred feet. Something catches Ozzie's eye, and he whips out his binoculars. "Can you hold your horses for a minute, Siku? I've got something down on Lost Lake."

Siku goes into a hover. "I'll give you ten seconds."

Gotta get some binoculars, thinks Benji, trying to follow Ozzie's gaze.

"There's your bear, Vicky," says Ozzie. "Triple Seven. Beatin' it across the water."

"You're kidding," she asks, fumbling for her binoculars. "Any cubs?"

Ozzie steadies both arms on his knees. "I can't tell. . . . No . . . wait. . . . There's something on her back. . . . Might be a cub . . . maybe two. . . . Too far. . . . Can't be sure. . . ."

"Any collar?"

"Can't tell . . . might be a cub clamped on to it. . . . Hah . . . smart cub."

"Time's up, guys," says Siku.

"Can I see those?" asks Benji, reaching for Ozzie's binos.

"Sure."

All Benji sees is a shrinking speck on the water. "You saw cubs?"

"I think so."

So Triple Seven's a mom, thinks Benji. It must be tough raising a family out here.

"That cub's toast," says Ozzie, suddenly seizing the binoculars and aiming them back at Fortune Creek.

Vicky sits up with a jerk. "Can you see it?"

"No. Willows too thick. I just caught a glimpse of Buster heading back upstream where he dropped it."

"Sorry, folks," says Siku. "No turning back now."

CHAPTER 10

LUNCH BREAK

That which you observe is in turn influenced by the tools
   of observation.
—*Werner Heisenberg, Physicist*

Soon after seeing Buster head up Fortune Creek toward the wounded cub, eagle-eye Ozzie makes another disturbing wildlife sighting. "I hate to tell you this, Siku, but we're being tailed by a pissed-off peregrine."

Siku whips off his sunglasses and looks over his right shoulder. Benji follows his gaze. He glimpses a razor-winged bird taking potshots at the helicopter's tail. It gets closer with each dive.

"What's in *his* shorts?" he asks.

"It's a her," says Ozzie. "A mother peregrine falcon. Thinks we're a predator too close to her nest. Probably on that cliff. Siku, boot it outta here or she'll attack."

"Gun it," says Vicky.

"I can't go any faster with the fuel we've got."

"Higher then. That'll shake her."

"Sorry. No fuel for that either."

"You gotta land then," says Ozzie. "Let her cool off. Or she'll take a piece out of your tail rotor.

"Ouch," says Benji.

"Double ouch," says Siku. "With a buggered tail rotor we'd spin like a top till we hit the ground." Siku does a quick scan of the terrain below, then plunges the helicopter toward a pile of square boulders near the cliff edge. "Hang on, folks. I'm gonna try and set our damaged side on one of those babies."

And, by the skin of Benji's grinding teeth, so he does.

Ozzie and Benji sit on a table-smooth rock near the cliff edge. A gusty north wind blows in their faces. Ozzie scans the Fortune Creek valley with his telescope while Benji chucks rocks at the boulder field far below. Vicky and Siku are in the damaged helicopter talking to Saber camp about an escape plan.

"Getting a feel for the tundra?" asks Ozzie.

"Yeah, a real crash course."

Ozzie chuckles. "Did you pack a lunch?"

"Nope. My dad said it was just another joyride."

"Fear not. I always carry emergency rations."

"Not more marshmallows."

"Always. But that ain't all." Ozzie pulls out a pastrami and rye sandwich that could easily feed three people. He rips it apart and offers half to Benji.

"Thanks." They eat in silence until Siku walks over.

"What's the plan, man?" asks Ozzie.

Siku pulls a tiny pair of binoculars out of his sealskin vest and starts glassing around. "They're bringing me a new float. Slinging it under the geologists' chopper. Could be another four hours, so get comfortable, boys."

"Great," says Benji.

lunch break   113

Ozzie looks at him. "Hey. Some rich German tourist would pay an arm and a leg to be in your shoes."

"Sure." This is Benji's first visit to the snow-free tundra. He likes the funny-shaped, knee-high shrubs everywhere. They remind him of San Francisco's Japanese Tea Garden, where his mother often took him as a kid. But he just can't get his head around the *size* of it all. And something about that boulder field gives him the creeps. A cold gust of wind slaps his face, and he shivers. "What I'd do for my CD player."

"You seemed pretty interested in that bear."

"But where is it now?"

"There it is," says Siku.

Benji stands up. "Buster?"

"Nope. That crazy bird."

"Where?"

"Perched on that big pointy rock."

"There's an awful lot of pointy rocks down there," says Benji.

Ozzie whips his scope around and finds the bird in an instant. "Check it out, Benji."

At first Benji sees only black circles through the telescope. "What bird?"

"Move your eye closer," says Ozzie.

"Whoa," says Benji when he finally sees the falcon. Her creamy breast shows up clearly against the gray boulders.

"I've heard her calling since we landed," says Ozzie. "Can you hear it?"

Benji looks up from the scope, straining his ears. "Kind of a crybaby call?"

"That's it." Ozzie cranks the scope to sixty power. "Try this."

Even from way up here Benji can see her ebony beak opening and closing with each plaintive cry. "She still looks mad."

"We gotta get you some binoculars." He waves his half-eaten sandwich at Benji. A big hunk of pastrami falls out of it and lands in some mud. He picks it up and stuffs it into his mouth, dirt and all. "This is the way field biology used to be. Before satellites, cell phones, and GPS's took over. All you needed was a tent, binos, scope, a bit of food." He takes another huge bite from his sandwich. "You found a nice perch like this. You waited. You watched. You listened. You let Mother Nature call the shots. If you got into trouble, you walked out."

As if on cue, five trilling notes float up from the valley floor. "You see?" says Ozzie. "Once you turn off all your toys, things start jumping out of the woodwork."

Benji looks up from the scope again. "Was that one of those squirrely things?"

Ozzie snorts into his beard. "White-crowned sparrow."

"Huh?"

"A dickeybird," says Siku.

Ozzie suddenly holds up his palm. The sparrow sings again. "You hear it? It's saying, *I-gotta-go-wee-wee.*"

Siku throws his head back for a silent laugh.

"What do you call that bird in Inuktitut?" asks Ozzie.

"Beats me," says Siku.

"Thought you grew up on the land, hunting, fishing, drinking Labrador tea and all that good stuff."

"Sure did," says Siku. "But birds are birds to me. They're all the same . . . except the ones I can eat. I can hear *those.*"

Just then a birdlike trilling sound escapes from somewhere in Ozzie's vest. Siku lifts his mirror sunglasses. "You got a bird stuffed in there?"

Ozzie doesn't answer. He's wrestling with a stuck zipper on a side pocket. The trilling continues in short spurts.

"You better get him out of there before he pees on you," says Benji. Siku laughs again.

The zipper finally lets go. Ozzie pulls out a cell phone not much bigger than his thumb.

"Oz here . . . Hey, kid. Whadya doin'? . . . You saw what? . . . Good spotting . . . Whadya have for lunch? . . . Popcorn and gummy bears! . . . Okay . . . You had a sleepover? . . . I love you, too. . . ." Ozzie puckers up his big hairy lips and plants three kisses on his cell phone. *Smack, smack, smack.* "And here's one for Momsy." *Smack.*

Ozzie flips the phone shut and crams it back into his vest.

Benji gives him a funny look. "That was your kid?"

"Yep."

"How many?"

"Just one. He's six. Said he saw a spider eat an ant."

"He called to tell you *that?*"

"Yep. He likes that kinda stuff."

At least he's interested in his dad's work, thinks Benji. "You brainwash him?"

Ozzie laughs. "I take him in the bush now and then. I wish I could more."

"Why don't you?"

"That's the only thing I don't like about this work. These six-week stints in the field eat up a lot of daddy time. Work gets in the way, you know."

"Boy, do I ever. Seems the richer my dad gets, the less time he has for anything." Benji thinks for a moment. "Why don't you get your kid to come out here?"

"Let's just say I don't have your father's connections. Think you'll be running this mine some day?"

"That's what *he* says."

"And you?"

"How should I know? I might do something with computers."

"Or aircraft?"

"Maybe."

"How about bears?"

"Hah! Be a scat sniffer like you?"

Ozzie laughs and goes back to his telescope.

Benji absentmindedly rubs his belly. "Were you kidding about those marshmallows?"

An hour later, Ozzie is still glassing around. Benji is lying nearby in a patch of dry moss with his X-Men ball cap over his face. Vicky has woken up from a long nap and starts quizzing Ozzie about what he's seen.

"Zip, I'm afraid. Unless you count that falcon, a couple bunnies, and a white-crowned sparrow."

"It's bears I'm looking for. Especially Triple Seven. I can't believe she gave us the slip again. Did you check the lake? The creek? The boulder field?"

The fired-up tone in her voice makes Benji lift his ball cap. Vicky's knuckles are almost white as she clutches her field book and paces back and forth. Her eyes sweep restlessly up and down Fortune Creek valley.

Ozzie cocks his head toward her. "Nothing personal, Vicky, but what's with you and Triple Seven? You collared her almost a year ago, and since then you've been following her every move."

Vicky stiffens. "What do you mean?"

"We've already got a ton of data on her. Where she dens. How far she travels. Home range. We even know what her meat caches look like—you know, the way she likes to dress them up with willows." Ozzie laughs. "I bet we've bagged and analyzed over a hundred scats from Triple Seven alone. Do you ever ask yourself how much is enough, Vicky?"

"She's slipperier than the rest of our collared bears." Vicky turns to Siku, who is sitting on a boulder chewing on a toothpick. "Houdini. The escape artist. Isn't that what you call her, Siku?"

"Fits, doesn't it?" he says.

Benji sits up. "Great for the helicopter business, eh, Siku? You taxi these guys around all day looking for The Incredible Vanishing Bear."

"Don't tell your dad, kid," he says with a grin.

"Sure, Ozzie," says Vicky. "I can sit at my computer and map her daily movements. I can tell you how fast her heart is beating, her temperature. I can even tell if she's running or . . ."

"Giving birth to cubs," adds Ozzie.

"That, too. I guess we proved that today." She looks fondly down at the lake.

"And now that cub's dead," says Siku flatly.

She flashes Siku a cold look. "There's the two other cubs." She turns to Ozzie. "You confirmed that on the lake."

"Can't be sure," Ozzie says. "Kinda hard to study bears when you're a thousand feet up flying full speed in the opposite direction with a crazy falcon on your ass."

"What's your beeper box telling you now?" asks Benji.

"Hardly any signal," says Vicky. "She couldn't be that far away already. Battery's dead, I think."

"On strike, you mean," says Siku chuckling. "Can you blame it, the way you work that thing?"

Vicky frowns. "We're using the best technology. The latest telemetry receivers. The most advanced satellites. State of the art biomedical collars equipped with GPS transmitters. Not to mention your fancy new helicopter."

"When it works," says Siku, grinning at Benji.

Vicky ignores him. This lady's on a roll, thinks Benji. "We've got the best tools—yet I always feel like I'm just one step behind her. How often have we seen Triple Seven since she left her den five weeks ago? Once. Today. That's it. She's tearing across the lake, we're limping home in a trashed helicopter." Vicky flips a stone over the edge of the cliff with her boot. "We fly all over homing in on her signal, then—poof—she's gone. Behind a rock. In the willows. Underwater—I don't know. Where do you hide in this bald country? Sure, we can tell where she's been, even where she's pooped, but never what she's actually *doing* at any moment."

Benji looks down at the lake wondering how a mother grizzly mourns her lost cub.

Vicky's voice softens almost to a whisper. "I'd give anything just to see her grazing down in that meadow, fishing in the creek, hunting a caribou or maybe nursing her cubs. But she won't let me near her. She won't let me see her natural behavior in the field."

Ozzie cuts in. "Forgive me, Vicky, but how do you expect to see her *natural* behavior if we're breathing down her back in a helicopter?"

"It's just one tool, Ozzie. A stepping stone. First we find her. Then we watch her to find out how she really scratches out a living in this barren place. How is anyone supposed to protect these bears if nobody knows how they really live?"

Benji tries to lighten her up. "But who's going to protect them from biologists?"

Ozzie waves the back of his hand at Benji.

Vicky carries on. "I don't care if we're working for miners or bunny-huggers. If we can't study these bears in their natural state, we might as well be at the Winnipeg zoo."

"We've watched lots of other bears," says Ozzie. "Seen them hunting caribou, digging up squirrels, swimming through rapids . . ."

"Attacking helicopters," says Benji.

Ozzie chuckles. "Remember those two we saw mating on top of the biggest esker north of sixty? Now *that* was an interesting assignment!"

"You did?" asks Benji.

"Helps keep the bugs down," says Siku.

Ozzie slaps his knee.

"Sure," says Vicky, "we've had some luck with other bears. But none live so close to the diamond mine. And none have cubs, at least that we know of. Triple Seven's a special bear, and we'll find her." Vicky walks right up to Ozzie and pokes his chest with a finger. "You asked me how much is enough? I'll track that bear till I get a real good look into her world. If I have to, I'll track her every day till the money runs out."

"Or her collar falls off," says Siku.

Vicky darts Benji a peculiar look, as if she just remembered whose son was listening.

"My dad could shut you down like *that,*" says Benji snapping his finger. "You spend weeks combing this moonscape for the Great Triple Seven and barely catch one glimpse of her. Another bear you weren't even looking for nearly trashes your chopper. What do I say if my dad asks how the bear hunt's going?"

"Tell him . . . tell him it's like finding diamonds. You spend a lot of time and money looking for them, but it's always worth it in the end."

"Is it?" asks Siku.

Ozzie sighs, then returns to his scope for his hundredth sweep of the valley. "I'll take another good look, Vicky. You never know where you might find her."

A few minutes later the wind stiffens, shaking Ozzie's telescope so badly he can't see a thing. Benji has been trying Ozzie's binoculars with zero success. Soon a stinging rain is upon them, and the four bear hunters dash for cover in the wounded helicopter.

MIDSUMMER

CHAPTER 11

CARIBOU COLUMN

The empty tundra may appear a drab and barren place, but let one caribou trot onto the skyline of an esker and the land comes alive.

—*George Calef,* Caribou and the Barren-Lands

July 10. The hilly country twenty miles east of Saber Mine.

A warm, frisky breeze gets the tundra shrubs swaying and glistening in the bright morning sun. The flare-up of tundra flowers is already over. Small, green berries begin to swell.

In the blink of an arctic spring, the frenzied songs and courtship displays of all the birds give way to the protective clucks of mothers minding their newly hatched young. A female ptarmigan, once white as snow, is now invisible against the speckled tundra floor. She purrs softly at her six chicks following her closely through thickets of dwarf birch. Feeding on the birch is a gray arctic hare whose white feet are the only reminders of a long-gone winter. It snips off tender new branches with its razor teeth. Suddenly hopping for cover, it flips back its ears and squints into the sun at the silhouette of three approaching grizzlies, a large female and two cubs.

The mother bear's phenomenal fat supplies laid on last fall are burnt. Her fast-growing cubs, though beginning to toy with morsels of scavenged meat and old berries, still nurse ravenously, milking away precious nutrients from their mother's thinning body. With the large male cub now dead, the other two feel freer to nurse whenever and wherever they like.

The rabid fire of hunger burns in the big bear's every cell. Where are the caribou that the bear's instinct and knowledge have promised summer after summer?

Both cubs scratch and whine at her heels, signaling their need for yet another nursing session. She ignores them and plods on through the shrubs to an open patch of ground sparsely covered with crowberry plants. She tries a few of the budding berries. They are still hard and bitter, but she crunches them down anyway. She walks to the edge of the clearing and sniffs a pink-flowered liquorice root, tucks her long claws into the soil behind it, and rocks backward. The sod gives way, like a giant golfer's divot. She peels back a thick slab and flips the plant upside down. Next, she sifts away the sandy soil with her claws and nibbles off a few sweet roots.

Not much of a meal for a hungry grizzly, but when the caribou aren't around, this kind of nip and tuck feeding goes on all day. Some roots here, horsetails there, a vole, a lemming. This time of year she may eat some tiny chicks after stumbling on their well-hidden nests. And, if she's lucky, the odd ground squirrel or two.

Luck is with her today. A ground squirrel has been watching the bear family for some time from the other side of the clearing. The many tunnel entrances to its underground home are shrouded by bushes, and the blustery winds have so far kept its scent from the bears.

The bear's digging triggers alarm in the squirrel, but instead of dashing down its hole, it runs into the open to see what's going on. The squirrel shoots up on its hind legs, just like a mini-grizzly bear, with its front legs hanging limp from its chest. It stands perfectly still except for its black-tipped tail, which it waves around. It drops back onto all fours and blurts out a shrill cry of alarm. *Sik-sik, sik-sik.*

Almost before the sound stops, a second squirrel answers from somewhere underground, then two more. The first squirrel dashes down a tunnel. The whole colony is now on full alert for immediate danger.

The cubs are hot on its tail. They crash into the shrubs, then race around, cramming their muzzles deep inside each hole. Their mother comes over and bats them out of the way. There's work to be done, some meat to be eaten—if she's lucky.

The squirrel colony is honeycombed with tunnels and peppered with holes. The big bear moves from hole to hole, sniffing each one carefully. With her fully healed nose she finds the most promising scent, then throws herself at it. Dirt and rocks fly out behind her. Like a dog, she digs sometimes with one paw, sometimes both, removing huge pawfuls of debris with each swipe. Soon, half her body disappears down the rapidly growing crater.

She stops occasionally for a good sniff or pulls her head out to make sure a squirrel doesn't try escaping through another hole. This goes on for half an hour until she climbs out and starts thumping on the colony's roof. She uses this trick, learned from her mother years ago, to shake the underground burrow, scaring the daylights out of the squirrels and making them run for it.

The cubs find this irresistible and join in the jumping. The trick works and three ground squirrels dash out of the very hole she has been digging.

The cubs scramble after them but trip over each other and end their game in a ball of flying claws and teeth. It's no game for their mother, who leaps over her cubs and madly chases the squirrels across the clearing. Despite their short, spindly legs, the squirrels put up a good race. Two of them disappear beneath the birch before she can grab them. The other leads the bear in a wild zigzag chase until it suddenly spins around, runs right through her legs and dives back down another hole.

The big bear is about to start digging all over again when a wisp of some new scent tickles her nose. It's a sweet horsey smell blowing over a high, rounded ridge to the north. She immediately springs to her hind feet. Her cubs do the same—they're getting quite good at this. She sniffs. They sniff. She slowly waves her head back and forth. So do they. She gets it. They don't. Caribou.

Between the bears and the ridge is a wide creek that snakes through a wide sedge meadow. The muddy banks of the creek are crisscrossed with countless caribou trails. Not an animal is in sight. But the big bear knows they are coming. The caribou are coming. Lots of them.

She takes another deep sniff, then breaks into a gallop for the creek. The cubs bound after her, sniffing the air, struggling to remember that scent. It has been weeks since they smelled a caribou, and they were so young then, so new to the world.

The mother bear jumps right into the creek without slowing down, but halfway across, she suddenly springs to her feet to peer up the ridge. The creek is too deep for the cubs to stand, and they swim circles around her while she looks for her favorite prey.

There. At the crest of the ridge. The prickly crown of a large bull caribou breaks the horizon. It prances into view, stops, then looks over its shoulder. Another caribou trots up beside it. Then another. And another. Soon there are over fifty caribou milling around at the top of the ridge. They are restless. None of them graze. They bunch together, stomping the ground with their front feet or shaking a rear leg out behind them.

Traveling with this column of caribou, in numbers only physicists understand, is an army of blood-sucking, flesh-boring, face-buzzing, brain-numbing bugs. Mosquitoes, blackflies, warble flies, nose botflies, all harassing the caribou in the heat of this midsummer day. The windswept ridge offers relief from the biting hordes, creating a temporary dam in the river of caribou now aimed straight at the bears.

Some nasty insect bite or antler jab in the rump sparks the leading bull into motion. It vaults over the side of the ridge and gallops toward the creek. Instinctively, the other caribou follow. The trickle of animals turns into a flood till there are hundreds of them streaming over the top of the ridge like buffalo of the tundra. Within minutes, over two thousand caribou have fanned out across the meadow. They graze fitfully between bug attacks.

The bugs and wind are in the bears' favor. The bugs keep the caribou distracted. The wind blows from the caribou to the bears. They are totally unaware of grizzlies in their midst. Beside a deep caribou trail on the opposite side of the creek, the mother bear crouches and waits under cover of some willows. At the sight and smell of the caribou, her cubs are beside themselves with excitement, but she cuffs them into silence every time they act up. As hungry as the big bear is, she knows it's only a matter of time before the caribou cross the creek.

A calf is the first to poke his nose in the water. It takes a few playful steps into the creek before the mother caribou gives a loud nasal grunt, beckoning it up the bank. The mother bear almost has to sit on her cubs to keep them from bursting out of the willows after it.

A few caribou begin crossing the creek farther upstream. The bear leans forward for a better view, watching them as they timidly high-step their way into the water, then trot out of the shallows on the other side like newborn colts. Soon the creek seems more full of caribou than water.

Several big bulls charge down the creek bank directly across from the bears. The mother bear gets ready to spring. She waits till they are all neck-deep in water, then leaps on the largest bull as a leopard might jump from a tree on an antelope.

The caribou bellows in terror and rakes its sharp antlers behind him trying to stab the bear's face. The bear clamps its hind legs around the caribou's neck and rolls headfirst off his back. This twists the caribou off its feet but its deadly antlers still thrash the air.

The bear keeps its whole head and shoulders safely underwater while trying to pull the caribou down with it. The instant the bull's head goes under, the bear whips around and grabs its nose between her teeth. She starts dragging him out of the water. The bull delivers a few solid kicks to the bear's stomach, then struggles to its feet. The bear shakes the bull so savagely by the nose that he is thrown on his back. After a couple more kicks, the shallows of the creek run red as the bear rips open the caribou's throat.

The cubs join her and the three of them enjoy the salty, satisfying tang of fresh blood. She rips off a mouthful of meat. For a tundra grizzly, this is the taste of life.

Her banquet, however, is rudely interrupted. While dragging her prize up the bank, she suddenly drops it, lifts her head, then springs up on her hind legs. Her forelegs hang limp and motionless in a begging pose.

Both cubs turn to look at their mother. They watch her every move. She sniffs deeply in several directions, dissecting the air for some new scent that makes her hackles rise. She lets out a gravelly growl that rumbles along the ground and electrifies the cubs' attention. She drops abruptly and grunts a quick command to them. The female cub instantly gallops toward her. The runt gives a rebellious snort. He wants to play with her kill. She barks at him again, and he reluctantly falls in line behind her. Then, without another look at the virtually untouched caribou, she turns her back to it and bolts.

She sprints a few paces, jumps to her hind feet, then sprints again. They all move like this for several minutes.

He's back: the giant male who killed her firstborn cub. Like the wolves and wolverines, like the foxes and ravens, he has been following the caribou wherever they go. And now their paths meet again. But she still can't see him.

Far from the creek and her kill, the mother bear stands once more and sniffs. The cubs stand around her feet, each with one paw on her leg as if propping her up. Finally, she spots the invading grizzly.

It's him all right. That sour, musky smell is unmistakable. He, too, is standing and sniffing, looking right at her. His muzzle and forepaws are smeared red. He has claimed her kill. Stolen it out from under her nose. She turns tail on the thief and runs away without looking back.

CHAPTER 12

STAKEOUT

The bear has powerful medicine to read your thoughts and know
your actions, so if you get into trouble with one, it's no one's
fault but your own.
—*George Blondin,* Yamoria the Lawmaker

July 16. A few miles away.

It looks quite out of place, this lonely mound of volcanic rock
that rises like a dark castle above a huge boulder field. Plopped on
top of this hill are three tents: two yellow dome tents, and a big
canvas wall tent. There are no shrubs to tie them to, and there is
no soil to bang in stakes. So, like the caribou skin tents of old,
they are anchored to the spot with a ring of heavy rocks. Still, the
tents strain at their roots as a stiff arctic wind hammers away at
them. There's no water up here either, just lots of wind and a
wide open view.

As if it weren't windy enough, a black helicopter with a yellow-
striped tail almost caves in all three tents as it comes in for a landing right beside them. Slung below the chopper is a barrel full of
water that Siku pumped from a creek far below.

Benji emerges from one of the dome tents with his fingers in his ears. His father has what he calls "serious meetings" at the mine over the next few days and encouraged Benji "to join the bear people for a little outing." Hah. Little outing, thinks Benji as he watches the chopper come down. I might as well be on Pluto.

Long before the rotors stop spinning, Vicky pops out of the cook tent and runs toward the helicopter. Benji follows, hungry for any kind of distraction in this bleak place.

Vicky flings open Siku's door. "Did you see any bears?"

Siku is writing in his logbook.

He raises a finger without looking up. "Wait a sec." He scribbles some more, then closes his book with a bang and a chuckle. "Sorry, Vicky, no bears. But do enjoy the water. I just calculated what it cost you to airlift it way up here. With all that farting around down by the creek, trying to find a place to land in those boulders, it'll run you about a dollar per gulp."

Vicky frowns. "Well, you can send the bill to Ozzie if we don't find that bear. He guaranteed me results if we camped here. I'm giving him three days and three nights, not a minute more."

"Then what?" asks Siku

"Then we'll just have to intensify our telemetry work. More computer mapping. More aerial searches . . ."

"More scat collection?" asks Benji.

"That, too. We'll do whatever it takes to find Triple Seven and see what she's up to."

"Okay, boss," says Siku. "In the meantime drink lots while you're up here. I'll need something to keep me busy. Being water-boy, I mean."

"Can I fly with you next time?" asks Benji.

"Sure, kid," Siku grins. "Maybe you can even wash your socks or something to get more trips."

As Benji and Vicky head for the cook tent, Ozzie comes out holding two hunks of rye bread plastered with mustard. "Everything's in order, Vicky. Went through all our supplies, and we've enough food to stay up here a week."

"Three days and three nights, Ozzie," she reminds him. "That's it."

"Sure, Vic. But there's one problem. How do I make a sandwich with nothing but chicken in the meat cooler? You know I hate chicken."

"No pastrami?" asks Benji.

"None."

Vicky shrugs. "I guess somebody goofed. You like peanut butter?"

Ozzie looks doubtfully at his half-made sandwich. "Mustard and peanut butter," he mutters. "Hmm. Well, there's always a first time."

"Gross," says Benji.

For lunch, the four of them sit in the cook tent around a blue plastic picnic table, taking refuge from the wind.

"So what's wrong with chicken?" Benji asks Ozzie after casting a curious look at his multicolored sandwich.

"It's the stink," says Ozzie.

Vicky sniffs her chicken sandwich carefully. "This meat's okay."

"No, I mean the chicken coop. It stinks. The one I slaved in as a kid. My parents got the idea I loved chickens. So I got that job. My brothers piled hay while I shoveled chicken shit."

"Where did your parents get that idea?" asks Benji.

Ozzie laughs, then takes a huge bite of his sandwich. A big blob of yellow, brown, and white goo splats onto the picnic table. Ozzie scoops it off with his thumb and licks it clean.

"What's the white stuff?" asks Siku.

"Marshmallow spread. For emergencies." Ozzie loses himself in his sandwich. "You asked me something, Benji?"

"The chicken coop."

"Right. When I was a little kid I never knew where eggs came from. I knew it had something to do with chickens. So one day I chased a hen right into the coop. I guess I terrorized the others. When I squeezed in, they all came exploding out the door in my face. That's when I learned my first lesson about studying animals."

"Oh?" says Vicky.

"Patience. That's the best tool anybody can have for this work." Ozzie fires a quick look at Vicky. "So anyway I went back to that stuffy chicken coop and hid in the straw. I told myself I wouldn't come out till I saw with my own eyes where the heck eggs come from. It seemed like hours. I didn't move a muscle," Ozzie laughs, "except when I sneezed once. Finally, they started making these weird clucking noises and hunkering down on their nests. Then I saw one hen stand up and push something around with her beak. Something white. I jumped out of the straw and all the hens went nuts again. But I found the eggs. All their nests were loaded with them. They'd laid them right in front of my dumb kid eyes."

Vicky snickers, then jumps up to wash the dishes. Siku studies the end of his toothpick while Benji listens to the wind pounding the walls of the tent like a big fist.

Ozzie polishes off the rest of his sandwich in a couple of bites. He wipes his beard with his shirt-sleeve, then continues. "My mom was freaking out by the time I came home all covered in straw. 'Oswald! OSWALD!'" he shouts in a crackly woman's voice. "'Where have you been?!' She didn't get *really* mad. Maybe it was the look on my face or something in my voice. I guess if she'd yelled at me that first time, I wouldn't be here today. But soon after, my coop duties started . . . and my disgust for chickens."

For the first time this meal, Siku turns to look at Ozzie. With a deadpan face he asks, "So *that's* why we're up on this rock, to look for chickens."

Benji laughs. "You guys are bushed!"

Ozzie dabs some goo from his sandwich off the table and flicks it onto Siku's sunglasses.

"Nice story, Ozzie," says Vicky, "but what works for chickens may not work for bears. How can you be so sure we'll spot Triple Seven just waiting and watching on our butts? You call *that* science?"

"I call it the Pokey Patient Approach. We've tried your High Tech Cat-and-Mouse Approach all summer. How many times have we seen her? Once. Swimming into a thunderstorm."

Vicky crashes more dirty plates into the sink.

"I'm not knocking it," says Ozzie. "Thanks to her satellite collar, we know she's been hanging out on that boulder field for almost a week."

"How come?" asks Benji.

"This is the raunchiest bear habitat around here. Maybe ten blueberries per square mile. Grizzlies don't hang around places like this unless they're hiding from something. Maybe Buster's been roughing her up again, stealing her food, chewing on her cubs, and she figures he won't come looking here."

Ozzie puffs himself up, now adopting the voice of a hard-sell radio announcer. "You wanted to see the *real* Triple Seven doing her thing unmolested by biologists in the *real* arctic wilderness. Here's your big chance. A once-in-a-lifetime offer. Guaranteed results or your money back."

"Cute, Ozzie," says Vicky. "We'll try it your way. Three days, max."

"And three nights," he says rubbing his hands. "That's usually when the action begins."

"Right," says Vicky, slamming a soup pot into the dish rack. "Round-the-clock shifts with the telescope." She swings around and points a dripping yellow glove at Siku. "Keep the chopper on red alert. There's no electric fence out here, and you never know when trouble might hit. Especially with Buster lurking around."

"Whatever," says Siku.

"And don't go wandering off, kid," says Vicky, turning her glove to Benji. "We promised your dad we'd bring you back in one piece."

The stakeout begins. Vicky assigns Ozzie to cover the north side of the hill. She and Benji set up a telescope on the south side. It's windier here and Benji hopes there'll be fewer bugs. Already his ankles and neck are covered with blackfly bites.

"Nobody home," says Vicky after only a few minutes of glassing around. "Would you mind covering for me? I've got some bear data to crunch on my computer."

She seems helpless without all her fancy toys, thinks Benji. He's willing to give it a try. "What ya gonna pay me?"

"Free room and board," says Vicky, walking toward the cook tent. "Just two and a half more days. Then you can escape to the big city . . . and I can get back to some *real* work."

Benji can't see a thing. With the wind shaking the telescope, his view is nothing but gray wiggles. He tries Vicky's binoculars but his eyes soon hurt and he gives up.

Break time, he thinks, and heads into the cook tent to scrounge a snack. He finds Vicky checking voice mail on her cell phone. Benji tries a marshmallow and peanut butter sandwich. Hmm. Not bad.

"See anything?" Vicky asks after scribbling down a page of messages.

"Just Buster and Triple Seven honeymooning on the rocks."

Vicky snickers.

Benji wanders over to the helicopter and finds Siku sitting in the pilot's seat reading a dog-eared science fiction novel set in the year 2510.

"Any good?" asks Benji.

"Helps kill time," says Siku.

Benji finds Ozzie tucked behind a big rock, patiently waiting and watching for something to happen. Just like in the chicken coop, thinks Benji. "See anything?"

"A couple bunnies, one bull caribou, and a juvenile bald eagle."

"How can you tell it was a . . . whadya call it? A juvenile?"

Without taking his eye from the scope, Ozzie reaches into his backpack and pulls out his *Birds of North America.* "Page 184."

Half an hour later, Benji is still flipping through the bird guide while listening to loud music on his earphones.

Alone in the men's dome tent, Benji opens his eyes and checks his watch. Midnight. Yesterday's gale has blown itself out. The sudden stillness wakes him, an unsettling silence he'd never imagined possible—certainly not in San Francisco. His restless gaze falls on a shaft of sunlight igniting the tent's yellow ceiling. *Sunlight?* Benji'd heard about people going crazy under the arctic's midnight sun. He reaches for his CD player. No. He needs company.

Minutes later he is by Ozzie's side. All evening Ozzie has been looking and looking. The sun floats timelessly just above the horizon, filling the sky with a deep orange glow.

Benji takes a turn on the telescope. He's getting better at this. At least he can focus clearly. But there's nothing to see. Nothing but a plain of boulders. The midnight sun casts strange shadows behind them. Did something move? Benji rubs his half-asleep eyes and looks again. Was that a bear or mirages from a dream?

The shadows play tricks with his mind. Two shapes streak across the boulder stage. A bear and a boy. They fall together into the shadows. In his mind's eye, Benji probes the darkness and sees a third figure: his mother, sailing through the air, screaming. . . .

Ozzie suddenly stands and stretches his hairy arms to the sky. "Time for a marshmallow break?"

"Yeah, sure," says Benji, catching his breath.

"What's wrong? Did you see something?"

Benji fidgets with the diamond stud in his eyebrow. "Ah . . . nothing."

In the cook tent they discover Vicky slumped over the picnic table, asleep. Her sandy red hair smothers the pages of a thick software manual. They admire the screensaver images flashing by on Vicky's laptop computer. "Bears, of course," whispers Benji. They're all grizzly cubs in various adorable and cuddly poses: playing in the snow, nursing on a beach, swatting butterflies in a flower-filled meadow.

"Cute," Ozzie says out loud as he flips the lid closed.

Vicky groans softly, then wakes with a start. "What's that?" she mumbles as she bolts upright, rubbing her eyes.

"Cute," Ozzie says. "Your bear cubs."

Vicky races for the tent door. "Where? Can you still see them?"

"Nope. I turned off your computer."

It's 3:45 A.M., the third and final night on the hill.

Something wakes Benji from a deep sleep. He sees Siku lying silently in his sleeping bag, his eyes wide and unmoving. Ozzie is dead asleep beside him, and, for once, not snoring like a bear. An eerie calm envelopes the camp. Benji hardly breathes.

Siku suddenly tilts his head forward and closes his eyes as if straining to hear something. Ozzie grunts in the midst of a dream. He rolls onto his side, then releases a small explosion deep down in his sleeping bag. Benji screws up his nose at the wicked waft of toxic air. Soon Ozzie is snoring up a storm. Siku jabs him in the ribs.

Ozzie grunts and farts again as he wakes up.

"What's wrong?" whispers Benji.

"She's here," says Siku.

Benji rolls his eyes as if looking for someone else in the tent. "Who?"

"Triple Seven."

Both Benji and Ozzie sit up and look straight at Siku.

"Whadya see?" asks Benji.

"Nothing."

"Whadya hear?"

"Nothing."

"How do you know she's here?"

"She's here all right." Siku pauses, closing his eyes again. "She's scared."

"Of *what?*" asks Ozzie.

"Don't know."

Benji hears nothing but the toodling of a lone tree sparrow drifting up from the boulder field. Ozzie taught him that song yesterday. Then, sure enough, he hears a squeaky whine.

"All right!" Ozzie exclaims as he pumps his fist in a victory salute. "I knew we'd find her. That was one of her cubs."

"Looks like she found us," says Siku.

"How close?" whispers Benji.

"Sounds like it's paying the boss a visit," says Ozzie. "Mama can't be far." He peels back his sleeping bag to reveal a pump-action shotgun and a box of red and green shells.

At the sight of them, Benji sucks in his breath. "What are the green ones for?"

"Bear bangers. Supposed to scare 'em off."

"And red?"

"Last resort. Killer slugs." Ozzie carefully packs four shells into the gun chamber, three green, one red. To the tune of "Shortenin' Bread," he sings under his breath "One for the money, two for the show, three to get ready, and four to go." He motions to the tent door with his chin. "Let's have a look."

Benji slowly unzips the inner flap of the door. Halfway down, he lets go of the zipper as if it were sizzling hot. A few inches from his nose, on the other side of a flimsy nylon screen, he sees another nose, this one big, black, and wiggling like crazy. He freezes.

"Can you fire a banger out the door without getting your hand chewed off?" asks Siku.

Ozzie points the shotgun to the ceiling. "Forget the door. I'll go through the roof."

"Plug your ears, kid," says Siku, plugging his own.

Benji's hands are too numb to move. Before he can even find them, the big bear snorts, shakes its muzzle and lumbers out of view.

Ozzie grins at his tent mates, shrugging. "Must have been bad gas."

Vicky is supposedly on the late-night shift. But again she has fallen asleep over her computer. She wakes to a pounding noise on the cook tent wall. With eyes still closed she figures it's the wind. She opens one eye to check. That's odd. The pounding noise comes only from the wall behind her. Wide awake now, she looks over her shoulder. What she sees makes her cover her mouth with both hands to choke back a scream.

The back wall of the tent is in full sun. It outlines the perfect silhouette of a standing bear cub batting moths off the tent. Vicky looks on with a mixture of fear and scientific curiosity. She has never heard of bears toying with insects. The shadows of hundreds of moths are plainly visible. Still chilled from the night, they vibrate their wings and walk in tight circles to warm up.

The bear cub bats the tent, the moths take flight, and, one by one, they return to do their little dance right under the cub's nose. The cub whacks the tent again, and the performance starts all over.

Vicky is spellbound and begins taking notes to describe this playful drama. All fear is forgotten. At least, until another dark silhouette enters the scene. It is much larger. At last, Triple Seven. Another cub trails behind.

Vicky's pencil slips out of her fingers and falls to the bedrock floor. She automatically stoops to pick it up but freezes when she sees the mother bear suddenly stand. In her huge shadowed form, Vicky sees the outline of the satellite transmitter on her collar.

Triple Seven stands still for a few moments, leaning against the tent. Then she drops slowly to all fours. As she does so, one fore-claw catches in the canvas. Vicky watches it with horror as it makes a clean straight line from top to bottom, slitting the tent open like a can of sardines.

Just as the bear withdraws its claw, a veil of clouds slips in front of the sun. The shadow bears vanish. All Vicky hears is the pounding of her heart. Where are they? she thinks. Should I yell? Would Triple Seven see that as a threat to her cubs and come crashing through?

The gun. Where's the shotgun? Ozzie's got it. Then she remembers the other gun on a rack above the tent's flimsy aluminum door. She lunges toward it, knocking her laptop computer off the table. It lands on the bedrock with a loud crack. "Shit! My data!" she whispers.

Vicky gets down on her hands and knees and crawls to the door, not daring to look out its little window until she's got the gun loaded and ready to fire. She finds the shells beside the bug dope and loads a couple while still crouched behind the door. Wait a minute. That was red for bangers and green for slugs. No. Green for bangers . . .

A cub whines close to her ear. From here she can even hear the disturbed breathing of its mother. No time to check. Her hands shake as she closes the loading chamber and flicks off the safety button.

Clutching the gun in her arms, Vicky slowly stands to peek out the window. At that precise moment, the mother bear does exactly the same thing. As Vicky's eyes rise to the bottom of the window, they are met by the equally curious eyes of Triple Seven.

"Aaaaagh!"

Instead of attacking, the big bear calmly drops down and starts ambling away, back down the hill. The cubs break into a whining chorus and try to attach themselves to her big swinging bum.

Still holding the gun, Vicky slowly opens the tent door to watch. She is torn by a mishmash of feelings: the flood of fear that just engulfed her, the need to roust the men, the urge to sneak after the bears and watch them, watch them undisturbed in the wild.

The threesome moves with remarkable speed. Before Vicky can think to raise the camera around her neck, they disappear over the brow of the hill.

Three heads pop out of the dome tents at the same moment. Vicky notices that Benji looks white as a ghost. Before she can yell at him to stay put, the three bears reappear over the hill, now galloping straight for her.

Vicky freezes for a second, then levels her gun squarely at Triple Seven's chest, all the while saying, "No, no. I can't, I can't." With her cubs trailing close behind, Triple Seven comes closer and closer in a full-blown charge. A hundred feet, sixty, thirty. *"Please* be a bluff charge," she says even as her finger tightens on the trigger. Fifteen feet. *BOOM!*

It's a banger. But not from her gun. Ozzie beat her to it.

The mother bear doesn't even look around. She keeps on running. One cub comes so close to Vicky it brushes against her leg, almost knocking her over. The three of them race past her as if she wasn't even there. They tear through the fresh slit in the tent wall. They do a bumper-to-bumper collision inside the tent, halting just long enough for Triple Seven to have a quick disdainful sniff of human odors, take a chomp on Vicky's computer, then run out through a second hole torn through the back wall.

"What's *with* you?" Vicky shouts at the retreating bear.

Ozzie is shouting, too. Wearing nothing but teddy bear boxer trunks, he's pulling Siku out of the tent. "Get that thing going!"

Siku, too, is in his underwear. He bounds over the rocks and jumps into the helicopter. Before he can even turn it on, another bear comes bounding up the hill.

"It's Buster!" Ozzie yells at the top of his voice.

Benji's head disappears into the tent.

Vicky stands frozen by the cook tent door. She is momentarily paralyzed by the sight of the biggest tundra grizzly she has ever seen barreling full speed toward her. She snaps out of it in time to tilt her shotgun up and fire. There is only the crack of her gun. No big boom. Rats! A slug. So that's red for slugs, green for bangers. She makes this mental note even as Buster is almost upon her.

BOOM! Ozzie gets a second banger off but to Buster, it might as well have been a mosquito buzzing in his ear. He's hot on Triple Seven's trail and nothing will stop him this time . . . except maybe these yummy human smells. An arm's length away from Vicky he skids to a stop and springs up on his hind legs.

With morbid fascination Vicky watches his huge wet nostrils flare and twist about. He slowly swings his head, with eyes closed, sniffing all the scents leaking out of the cook tent. Fascinating, thinks Vicky, always the scientist. I've never known a bear to close its eyes when it sniffs. She sniffs, too. Last night's chicken burgers, hot chocolate, oranges. She also detects a distinct hint of marshmallows.

There is Buster, near enough for her to reach out and touch his dark matted fur and smell his sour breath. At this moment she's thinking not about pain and death but about whether she could safely raise her camera to get an incredible full-frame grizzly head-shot. Better not. As for *her* head, Buster could knock it clean off with one quick bat of his paw.

Instead he ignores her. After a couple more sniffs, the bear wheels around and turns his back to her. Something beyond the dome tents has caught his attention. It rouses an angry growl from deep in his throat. The helicopter.

With his heart pounding, Benji risks another peek out the tent door. Siku is cranking the helicopter to full throttle. Ozzie is doing his best to buy time. He waves his arms and jumps around, trying to distract Buster from eating his boss. Buster just stands there, glaring at the helicopter. Benji is afraid even to blink.

He watches Ozzie pump the shotgun. Is this the killer slug? wonders Benji. The answer comes a second later. Ozzie raises the barrel to the sky. *BOOM!* The bear glances up at a puff of orange smoke. "Are you deaf?!" Ozzie yells. "That's my last banger, pal. The next one's a slug."

Ozzie waves to Siku, his arm making frantic propeller motions above his head. "Get that toy flying, man!"

Benji sees Siku check something on the dash, then hold up one finger.

"No, no!" yells Ozzie. "Don't wait! Take off now!" Then Ozzie spots Benji with his head out the tent door. "No! Wait!"

he yells, pointing at Benji. "Take Benji!" He motions to Benji. "Go for it!"

Benji pops out of the tent and is about to make a mad dash for the chopper when he remembers what Ozzie once told him about running from a grizzly. "It's the stupidest thing you could do," he said. "Back away slowly or you're meat on the run." Then Siku's words barge into Benji's head. "Never approach a running helicopter without getting a thumbs-up from the pilot." So, wearing nothing but blue boxers, Benji hops *sideways* over the rocks, with one eye on a raging grizzly, another on a screaming helicopter. Above the roar he hears Ozzie yelling, "Don't make me do this, Buster. We're just harmless biologists. Nice bear. Shoo, bear! Shoo!" His shotgun is leveled squarely at the bear's head.

A few paces from the helicopter, Benji catches the pilot's eye. Siku flashes him a cool thumbs up, like everything is routine. Benji scrambles in beside him. The instant they lift off, Buster hits the ground running—straight for Ozzie.

"Ozzie! Look out!" yells Benji. At the moment Benji thinks Ozzie will fire, something yellow rolls between him and the galloping bear. Buster throws himself on it and starts tearing it to pieces. "It's Vicky's tent!" says Benji. "You blew it away. Did you *plan* that, Siku?"

"Of course," he says, now hovering directly above Buster. "Hit the siren, kid. I gotta keep my eye on this guy."

Benji pumps a big red button on the ceiling, the first thing Siku showed him during his flight lesson weeks ago. Below a hail of police blasts and hurricane winds, Buster goes on shredding Vicky's tent. Bits of yellow nylon blow over the edge of the hill. He rakes into her sleeping bag. Feathers fill the air. He chomps down on something hard and square. He gives it a shake in his teeth, as if skinning a ground squirrel, then lets go. "Whoa! Bad bear!" exclaims Benji as he watches Vicky's beloved telemetry box crash on the rocks.

Siku lunges at Buster again and again. The bear stands up, trying to slash at Siku's floats that taunt him just out of range.

Benji pumps siren blasts in his face. "This guy's unstoppable!"

"Keep on him," says Siku.

Ozzie backs away slowly, his shotgun still raised. Meanwhile Vicky moves in with her camera. Benji blasts away with greater gusto, as much to push Vicky out of danger as to scare off this maniac bear.

Siku storms Buster from the rear, trying to herd him off the hill. After one final slash at Vicky's tent, Buster gallops over the edge with Siku and Benji hot on his heels.

In twenty minutes it's all over. Siku and Benji are back on the ground. They chased Buster through the boulder field, finally leaving him five miles from camp. As usual, they saw no sign of Triple Seven and her cubs.

Still in his boxers, Benji hunches over the mangled remains of Vicky's tent, marveling at the claw marks in her sleeping bag.

"Why didn't you dart him?" asks Vicky the moment Ozzie emerges from his tent, now fully dressed.

Ozzie zips up his fly while nodding to the cook tent. "You had the dart gun, Vicky."

"Oh," she says, looking back at the ravaged canvas walls.

"Besides," adds Ozzie, "I don't think one dart could carry enough punch to bring Buster down."

"We could have collared him. . . . We could've." To Benji she looks genuinely sad.

"Hey," says Ozzie. "I promised you guaranteed results, didn't I? How could you top that show? Eyeball to eyeball with Triple Seven. You could've petted her cubs if you wanted. Buster posed nicely for you while swatting at the chopper. All that, without the use of mind-altering drugs!"

Benji hears Siku's muffled laugh from inside the remaining dome tent.

"Anyway, you can't go around collaring every bloody bear on the tundra," says Ozzie. "What's the point?"

Benji is thinking the same thing.

"Perhaps you're right, Ozzie. We might learn more about these bears through more intensive studies on the ones already collared."

"*More* intensive?" says Ozzie.

Vicky nods vigorously. "I agree, Ozzie. We need to really turn up the heat on our collared bears."

"Well, that's not *exactly* what I was getting at."

But he has lost Vicky's attention. She pulls out a carpenter's measuring tape and, with Benji's help, checks the width of Buster's claw marks. Ozzie retrieves the trashed telemetry box and flicks through various channels. He shakes his head as he hands it over. "I'm afraid your beeper box is dead, boss."

Vicky fondly strokes its slashed leather case. "No problem, Ozzie. This machine served us well. I ordered a new model last week. Should be in camp by now. It has almost twice the range as this one and combines satellite, radio, and GPS all in one box. It should make it much easier to find our slipperiest bears."

"Like Triple Seven?" asks Benji.

"Yup," she says with a determined clap of her hands. "It's been interesting trying it your way, Ozzie, but with improved technology I think the odds of finding her are now in our favor."

At this comment, Siku pokes out of the tent and rubs his palms together. "Looks like it's cat-and-mouse time again, folks."

CHAPTER 13

GHOST HUNT

Finding a bear out there is like finding a needle in a haystack.
—*Robert Mulders, Bear Biologist*

Two weeks later, far from the biologists' lookout, the collar falls off. As the mother bear rises, doing her giant seesaw stretch, it pops off her neck. She looks at it lying in a tea-colored puddle. She sniffs it, gives it a good crunching bite, then calmly walks away. Both cubs in turn do exactly as their mother, sniffing and biting the split collar like freshly downed prey. The female cub suddenly wheels around and bolts for her mother. The runt lingers over the collar, unwilling to leave it. He feels strangely vulnerable. After all, hasn't this thing provided a lifeline for him to cling to during more than one wild escape from danger? Before finally abandoning it, he gives the collar a few more sniffs, licks it gently, then pees on it.

It may have been those slashes from the falcon. Or maybe the breakaway part of the collar malfunctioned, the weaker section that's made to automatically decay and let the collar drop after three years—not eleven months. Maybe it broke too soon.

What does the bear care? The collar's gone. Good riddance.

Half a mile from where the collar dropped, the bear family beds down for a midday nap. The mother bear chooses one of several clumps of stunted spruce trees that hug the sheltered, southern slope of an esker. The trees offer some shade, and the tall grasses growing between them make for a smooth, dry daybed.

The mother wakes to the low, grunting conversation of caribou. Both cubs are already awake and want to nurse. They eagerly climb onto her chest but are spilled onto the grass as she stands up to steal a glance at the herd. She pokes her head above the spruce, then quickly hunches back down. The caribou are headed right for them. About thirty of them, mostly adult females and their month-old calves. They follow a deep caribou trail that parallels the esker.

The herd moves like an accordion—bunched together for a while, then strung out, then bunched again. They are fitful, stopping, violently shaking their heads, then dashing forward so fast they almost knock each other over. It's the bugs again. Mosquitoes and biting flies buzz about their faces and torment their legs and rumps.

The caribou haven't seen or smelled the bears. They're still upwind and thoroughly distracted by bugs. Their trail leads past the bears' little clump of trees.

The big bear crouches, belly down, limbs drawn in, flattening herself against the grass like a stalking lioness. Her cubs climb onto her back and whine, deprived of nipples. The hunting bear reaches behind and knocks them off. The cubs hush up and align themselves beside her in the same hunting pose.

The caribou trot closer. The big bear's nose twitches with the delicious scent of her favorite prey. She hears them snorting bugs from their noses and grunting to one another. Closer yet and she hears the *click, click, click* of their legs.

The lead caribou is almost upon them. It stops to sniff the air. Still upwind, she catches a wisp of some new scent that she can't quite identify. She takes another hesitant step closer and twirls her long muzzle around in a tight circle. Grizzly.

The caribou whips her head and shoulders back so fast that her front hooves are yanked off the ground. In the same breath, she rockets herself forward with a powerful surge of her hind legs. This leaping action triggers the release of a strong warning scent from her hind feet. It tells other caribou that danger is near. Turn back! But before her front hooves hit the ground, the bear blasts out of her hiding place.

The ambush works. The caribou is taken totally by surprise. Her killer bowls her over with a lunge, a leap and a quick, deadly bear hug around her hindquarters. She tries hopelessly to struggle to her feet. Her legs flail. Her head swings. The bear throws her full weight on top of the caribou and breaks her neck with one mighty bite.

The other caribou react as a unit. They stop at once but don't scatter. The adults lift their heads, sniffing and snorting. They paw the ground and crane their necks for a better view. The young ones bawl. A few restless caribou in the rear start pushing forward, then, like a stack of dominoes, they are all in motion again. They trot in the same direction, making only a little swerve around the kill site before clicking back onto the same trail.

Still parked on their former leader, the mother grizzly passively watches them go by as if they were so many clouds.

The bear rests for a minute, then starts dragging away the limp caribou. The cubs do their best to help, each grabbing a leg and jerking it along to the accompaniment of their fierce growls. Their mother effortlessly steers the heavy animal over several moss hummocks, through the dense spruce wall, and onto their grassy daybed.

This time nobody steals her prize. Almost half the caribou is eaten and the rest is perfectly camouflaged by the time the helicopter arrives. Like an arrow, it goes straight for the dropped collar, which has been transmitting all day with no bear attached to it.

The mother bear's heart beats furiously, set off yet again by that hateful sound. She spies on the helicopter through a thick screen of spruce.

She blinks one eye, then the other. At the same time, she slowly swings her head from side to side to confirm what she is seeing. The helicopter is black with yellow stripes along its tail. She remembers it well. It is alarmingly close, only a few hundred yards away, yet today it seems less threatening. It doesn't circle around like it usually does before an attack. It doesn't zoom back and forth overhead. It simply zeros in on the spot where the collar fell off, hovers for a moment, then drops to the ground.

Two humans climb out of the belly of the helicopter, a big hairy one and a smaller thin one. They bend low and run away from the noisy machine. The little human stops suddenly and throws its forelegs above its head. It is looking at something on the ground. The big human stoops over and picks it up. The bear squints. Yes, she can see it now, what they're so interested in. It's the collar she once wore.

The two humans face each other, seeming to communicate. The arms of the small one move quickly, almost in a blur. Above the roar of the helicopter, the bear can hear angry mouth sounds. They turn their backs to each other and raise something black to their eyes. They appear to be looking for something else.

Something far away. The little human returns to the helicopter, carrying the collar. The big human stays on, holding the black thing to his eyes and slowly turning round. When he faces the spruce trees lining the bottom of the esker, he stops turning. He points at something—the bears' hiding spot.

The big human dives back into the helicopter, which instantly takes off.

Like a burrowing ground squirrel, the big bear throws herself at the base of the spruce trees. Her cubs naturally do the same. The stout, lower branches provide just enough cover to conceal them all from probing human eyes.

The helicopter's shrill whine gets louder. It stalks low and slow. The big bear takes choppy breaths with long pauses in between. All the bears are master hiders. They have had much practice. They lie dead still except for the occasional tremor of fear that shakes the cubs. Not daring to lift her head, their mother follows the approaching aircraft with her deep brown eyes. The humans seem to be checking out each little clump of spruce where a grizzly might hide. The helicopter is now so close they can feel the terrible blast from its rotors.

It skirts the edge of their clump. The noise is deafening. The wind is maddening. Big hunks of moss and dirt start blowing off the top of the freshly built caribou cache. The bear warily eyes a caribou leg emerging from under the flying debris. It sticks out the side of the cache like a sore thumb. But the humans miss it. They fly so low, they can't see what's right below them. They miss the bears, too. For a few awful seconds, the helicopter hovers just above their heads. Then . . . it flies on. It doesn't stop. No sirens. No chase. No darts in the butt.

Half an hour later, the mother grizzly finally lifts her head and looks back to where the helicopter flew away. The sky is empty. She looks down at her two cubs sleeping in the dry grass. She swings her head around and takes a sniff of her meat cache, now fully her own. In the silence and safety of the moment, a flood of warmth fills her chest. Call it joy.

CHAPTER 14

DOUBLE BLIND

Miners came—digging and grubbing everywhere, not for good, wholesome roots, but for shiny yellow sand that they could not eat.

—*Ernest Thompson Seton,* King of the Grizzlies

Contentment pours from the bear through a great and gaping yawn. She floats freely on her back in the center of a small lake. Her forelegs drift lazily in front of her as she slowly sculls the cool, mirror-calm water. This motion sets the long blonde hair of her stomach swaying on the surface like seaweed in a gentle current. Her hind legs dangle in the depths. Occasionally, they churn the water in easy circles as if she were riding an underwater bicycle. This bear is completely at home in the water. She is a free-floating, back-swimming, tundra-dwelling hippopotamus.

Here she can escape the panting heat of the midday sun on this windless summer day. She rolls over on her belly to keep an eye on her cubs as they play rough-and-tumble games along the lakeshore. Now she is a crocodile. All but her eyes and nostrils are submerged.

The profound peace of the moment is broken by a lone mosquito crawling up her nose. The bear sneezes, blowing a great gush of bubbles below her. The disturbance on the lake draws out more mosquitoes. Soon a pesky cloud hovers about her face. She sinks. For a while she spends more time under the water than on it. Then she comes floating slowly toward her cubs, who are intensely absorbed in a jaw-wrestling contest. They don't notice her approach. Her claws finally touch bottom. Now she creeps into the shallows, coming within a few yards of her cubs. Still in crocodile mode, she watches them for a few minutes. The cubs silently chew on each other's faces in an ancient grizzly sport. Then *sploosh!* The mother bear erupts from the water in a playful burst of energy.

The cubs scatter, then dash back toward her, only to be doused in a wall of spray as she shakes. They want to nurse, but before all can settle, the mosquitoes find them. The mother bear instinctively leads her cubs to higher ground, where the bugs are usually less bothersome.

She stops on top of a high hill above the lake. It is thickly carpeted with cranberry, crowberry, and Labrador tea. Here and there are rounded humps of pink granite that break through the green carpet like a pod of surfacing whales.

The big bear sprawls on her back in a cushiony hollow, stretches all four legs into the air and waves them about. Then, with her legs still up, she grabs her hind paws with her front and pitches back and forth. The cubs move expectantly closer. She stops rocking and sits back against a smooth rock outcrop. She makes a soft murmuring sound in her throat, inviting her cubs to climb aboard. They scramble onto her furry belly, find a nipple, and suckle to their hearts' content. Within minutes, all bears are fast asleep in the sunshine.

The mother bear is woken by a weak buzzing noise. Till now, no insects have found them on the hill. No bugs buzz about her cubs still asleep on her chest. Nothing crawls up her nose or into her ears. There is just that one irritating noise that gradually gets louder. She snarls suspiciously while her searching eyes inspect her tundra kingdom. They stop and harden upon a dark speck above the southern horizon.

She stands abruptly, knocking her startled cubs to the ground. She stares at the fast approaching speck to confirm its identity. The cubs in turn stare at her, waiting for a sign. Their mother huffs as if to communicate, *Here we go again.* The cubs break out in pitiful whines. The bears flee down the other side of the hill.

It's becoming almost routine: humans dropping from the sky. The soft envelope of this calm summer day is torn open by another helicopter. The bears sprint for cover behind a big boulder near the bottom of the hill. They flush a rough-legged hawk that had been using the rock as a hunting perch. The cubs hide while the big bear cautiously peers around one edge waiting for the helicopter.

Here it comes, streaking over the lip of the hill. She doesn't recognize this machine. It is red with white markings on its belly and tail. She can make out the image of a bear on the side. It's a polar bear on the run.

The helicopter swoops in low and fast, flying straight toward their rock, then right past. It sails directly overhead without slowing down. The bears dodge to the other side of the rock. The humans must have seen them. But no. They fly on to a thin island of sand poking above a field of low shrubs. The helicopter lands there in a cloud of swirling sand, then shuts down.

double blind

When all is quiet, the cubs sneak a peak at the downed machine. Their mother gives a low growl under her breath, and they retreat behind the rock. The humans seem to be taking an awfully long time to get out.

The mother bear becomes curious. She crouches low and grunts a command for her cubs to follow. Together they slink into the dense shrubs and crawl forward to a place where she can study the humans more closely without being seen.

Three of them sit in the helicopter. She is close enough to see their mouths constantly opening and closing. Occasionally, they reach into an object on their laps then put something into their mouths. They must be eating.

Two humans finally climb out of the helicopter's belly. One throws something directly at the bears. He couldn't have seen them, but it flies right over their heads and lands in the bushes behind them. Before his mother can tow him back in line, the runt male follows his nose to whatever the human threw. He finds it lying on a patch of bright green moss.

He sniffs the thing. A rich, foreign sweetness fills his nostrils. It smells like cloudberries, only sweeter. Just as he is about to eat it, his mother bats him aside. She inhales the strange object's sugary scent. A faint human smell makes her snort and pull her head back. But the alluring sweetness is irresistible.

She rolls the thing around in her paw, inspecting it closely. It is white and cool and juicy and about one claw-length long. Each end has small patches of chewed red skin. One has something white and round hanging from it. (Unknown to the bear, it is a grocer's label: New Zealand—Grade A—Royal Gala Apple.) She takes one final sniff, imprinting this new scent on her brain, then downs the apple core in one mouth-watering gulp.

She swings round to face the sleeping helicopter, realizing that, for several minutes, she had her back to three humans who are dangerously close. Still crouching out of sight, the bear creeps closer, the same way she would ambush a caribou. Her cubs obediently move with her, sticking to her side. A squeaky whine leaks from the female cub, who is rewarded with a swift bat. The curious runt male tries standing. His mother knocks him flat. She stops creeping forward, tipping her head up just enough to see what's going on.

One human still sits in the helicopter while the other two dig up sand. They must be looking for food. Perhaps they know where to find more of those sweet morsels the bear just ate.

To the bear, they are digging very strangely. Instead of bending over and pulling sand away with their forelegs as she would, they stand, poking the ground with long sticks that have a wide point on one end. They appear far more interested in the sand than any roots or animals they might dig up. Each human has a white sack beside them into which they dump their sand.

One of the humans scoops up some sand, holds it close to his face, then makes excited mouth sounds to the other human. They both look at it closely. The bear can see the sand has a purple tinge to it. They carefully put this in a sack, then keep digging.

Sik-sik, sik-sik. The bear hears the alarm call of a ground squirrel. The cubs automatically stand up. Their mother woofs sharply and they dive back into the bushes. Both humans suddenly stop digging and look her way. She ducks. The digging sounds continue and she peeks her head up again.

She spots the squirrel running across the bald patch of sand. It stops right behind the humans and jumps to its hind feet. They don't even look at it. They keep digging and filling their sacks with sand. One more squirrel explodes from a tunnel right beside them. Then another. Soon the three of them stand side by side, as if in a chorus line, chirping away and waving their long black-tipped tails at the oblivious diggers. One thrust from a digging stick exposes the side of a tunnel. Another ground squirrel pops out and runs right through the human's legs.

This is too much for the watching grizzly. She knows how much work is involved in unearthing a ground squirrel, let alone catching it for a meal. And here, right before her eyes, are four of them virtually offering themselves to be eaten. Forgetting her fear of humans for a second, she springs to her full height to see where the last ground squirrel went. All that chirping got the cubs really excited, and they, too, bolt upright in full view of the humans.

At first the humans don't see the three bears. They dig on, stuffing their sacks. The squirrels see them all right and dive into what's left of their tunnels. One human looks over his shoulder to see what spooked the ground squirrels. Just a stone's throw away is a big blonde grizzly flanked on each side by a chocolate brown cub. He throws down his digging stick. A long, loud noise comes out of his mouth. The other human, making the same noise, frantically waves his forelegs. Then they both dash for the helicopter and jump in—the same way the squirrels disappeared down their holes.

Spurred by the sight of fleeing animals—both squirrels and humans—the runt male can't contain himself any longer. He leaps forward over the shrubs to get a piece of the action. Before he can poke his nose into the squirrel tunnels, a human jumps from the helicopter and runs over to retrieve his sacks of sand.

To the mother bear, the human's sudden advance can mean only one thing: he is threatening her cub. With a bellowing roar and slashing claws she drops to all fours and charges the human at full speed.

Her cub bawls. The human screams. It lifts one foreleg and points something at the charging bear's face.

A sticky orange spray plasters the bear's eyes, nose, and mouth. She can't see a thing. Her nose clogs shut. She coughs out hunks of orange goo. An instant later, the pain hits. A savage, stabbing pain that knocks her off her feet. She falls backward, almost landing on her squealing cubs. They try to lick the stuff off her face. Then they, too, are sent reeling when a scorching pain sets their mouths and throats on fire.

The mother bear hears frenzied human mouth sounds. Then the helicopter wakes up, making a low howling noise, then that awful rising scream. She feels the cubs tugging at her fur. When she tries to open her eyes, they fill with stinging sand swept up by the helicopter. Blindly, she staggers away from the hateful machine.

As the helicopter lifts off, she opens one eye just enough to see a long black thing poke out its side. The thing is glassy at one end. A human has his face pressed against the other. The long thing moves around, following the motion of the bears as they make a stumbling retreat into the meager safety of the shrubs.

CHAPTER 15

BLISSED OUT

Adopt the pace of nature, her secret is patience.
—Ralph Waldo Emerson

An hour later. The Saber Mine cafeteria.

"That's her!" says Vicky. "That's gotta be Triple Seven!" She clutches a digital photo taken from the geologists' helicopter. It shows three tundra grizzlies, a large blonde female and her two chocolate brown cubs. The adult is sprawled on her back with her forepaws pressed against her eyes. Her face is spattered orange from cayenne pepper spray. Her cubs cower beside her, their fur squashed flat by rotor-wash.

Ozzie looks over her shoulder, shaking his head. "That geologist used a whole can of bear spray on her."

"He's lucky to be alive," says Vicky. "Why would he leave the chopper with a bear just about knocking on their window?"

"He wanted those till samples real bad," says Siku, who is digging bacon bits out of his molars with a toothpick. "They hit pay dirt out there. Purple sand."

"Look at this, Vicky," says Ozzie. "He gave me a sample." He pulls a plastic bag from his vest and looks around for a safe place to dump it. He stuffs the rest of his cinnamon toast in his mouth, wipes his plate clean with his shirtsleeve, then covers it with purple sand. "Diamond indicator minerals."

Vicky reluctantly puts down the photo and zooms in with a twenty-power hand lens hanging from her neck. The purple sand resolves into the well-known mix of minerals that fills the dreams of diamond hunters: black chromite, olive-colored olivine, and purplish garnets that give the sand that special color. "Big deal," she says, turning back to the photo. "I've seen purple sand all over the place."

Siku darts a curious look at her over the rim of his coffee cup.

Vicky pushes the plate aside. "There's enough diamonds out there to put one around the neck of every woman in China. It's *bears* I'm after. And they're a lot harder to find." She shakes the photo near Ozzie's nose. "Exactly when was this photo taken?"

"Eleven fifty-five. Just before lunch."

Vicky looks at her watch. "Only an hour ago. Did he get a GPS hit on Triple Seven?"

"You bet. Marked his test pit long before she charged."

Vicky stands up suddenly, almost spilling her untouched bowl of tomato soup. "Great! We'll leave immediately. Ozzie, get her GPS coordinates. Siku, meet us at the chopper in five minutes. For all we know she could be miles away from the test pit by now. Step on it."

Siku slowly lowers his cup and studies the coffee grounds at the bottom. "I don't think so, boss."

Vicky leans over the table, trying to catch his eye. "You don't think *what?*"

"I don't think we'll be flying anywhere. Chopper's in pieces. Engineer's got the rotors off. Hundred-hour inspection time."

Siku finally looks up at her. "I told you last night we'd be grounded after lunch."

"No!" snaps Vicky, slamming her field book on a plate of crackers. "You're not serious. This could be our last chance to slap that new collar on Triple Seven before winter comes. How much time before your machine's back together?"

Siku shrugs. "I'll introduce you to my engineer. Ask her."

Vicky is about to blow a fuse. She gives Siku a searing look, then scoops up her field book, leaving a trail of smashed crackers behind her. She is about to dash out of the cafeteria when Ozzie politely steps in front of her path with both palms up.

"Wait a second, Vicky. Before you tear a strip off Siku's engineer, I've got a solution. We take the Beaver."

"A fixed-wing? What good is that? Have you ever tried darting a grizzly from an airplane going a hundred miles an hour?"

"Yes, actually. A total flop. That's not what I'm suggesting. There's lots of lakes to land on. Once we find Triple Seven, you dump me off nearby. I keep an eye on her while you guys get the chopper. It'll be back together by then. What do you think?"

Siku claps his hands. "Goof-proof plan, Ozzie boy."

Vicky's not so sure. "How do you know we'll find her?"

"Trust me, Vicky," says Ozzie puffing up his chest. "I'm your assistant field flunkie, aren't I? You got a better plan?"

Vicky tightens her lips, nods once, twice, then a whole bunch of times. "Okay, Ozzie. We'll try it your way . . . again." She wheels around to Siku. "We'll meet you on the runway in ten minutes."

"I Roger that," says Siku.

Two hours after the bear photos were taken, they find Triple Seven, without hardly looking. After buzzing the test pit where the geologists had been digging, they fly in wide circles around it. Ozzie spots a large, glistening object moving along a high esker. The mirrorlike flashes off her sun-bleached coat catch his eye. "Look at her!" he exclaims. "She looks like a piece of glass shining on the hillside."

"Got it," says Siku as he instinctively pulls the nose up—he doesn't want to scare her—and brings the bear over to Vicky's side.

"Finally!" shouts Vicky. "There she is!"

Siku turns the volume down on his headset.

"Where do you want to be dumped, Ozzie?" asks Siku.

"Try Bliss Lake dead ahead. If she sticks to this esker like I think she will, she'll run right into it. Dump me on the far shore by that beach. I can watch her from there."

Unseen by the bears, Siku drops down to Bliss Lake, landing in a cloud of spray beside a sickle-shaped beach. "Bring your bathing suit?"

"Later, man. Maybe after all the darting and poking and collaring is over. Get the heck outta here before she shows up."

Ozzie is on the pontoon with all his gear before the plane touches the beach. Siku skillfully feathers the prop to bring the plane sideways onto the beach. Ozzie jumps off and signals two thumbs up. By the time the floatplane lifts off, he's unfolded his camo-colored lawn chair, got the telescope set up, and is already glassing around.

He keeps swinging his scope back to the esker where they saw the bears. Like a giant snake, it reaches halfway across the narrow lake and ends abruptly in a steep, sandy slope.

The plane's drone fades and soon Ozzie is wrapped by an awesome silence as thick as it is wide. Ozzie is in his element. No sound, no motion goes undetected. Even his nose, as limited as a human nose is, stays on high alert for any unusual scents. He occasionally looks up from his telescope and glances all around. Ozzie knows that the bears could easily find him before he finds them.

A few minutes later he detects a faint splash and a ring of ripples on the lake. Something drifts out in the middle. He zooms in on the dark gray back and striped neck of a red-throated loon. Its head looks unusually droopy. In the bright sunlight reflected off the water he can clearly see the ruby-red sheen of its eyes. The loon droops its head some more, then swings it to rest on the feathery pillow of its back. With his scope on full power, Ozzie watches the red eyes blink, slower and slower, until they finally close in sleep.

Half an hour passes. Ozzie watches a herring gull glide by, hears a cascade of pebbles trickle into the lake, smells the musky scent of fox somewhere near him. He drinks it all in. His senses are keen. His concentration unbroken. His breathing relaxed. He listens. He watches. He occasionally sniffs the air. Immersed in the heart of a timeless, boundless land, he patiently, joyfully waits.

Then it comes. A cry of alarm cuts the silence like a knife. *Ya-wow, ya-wow, ya-wow.* Ozzie instantly recognizes the squealing call of a parasitic jaeger. He slowly stands and tips back his Saber Mine cap. The call comes from somewhere above the esker. He clamps his binoculars to his eye sockets and begins a slow systematic sweep.

At first, the only motion he sees is the wiggling of heat waves that blur the boundary between land and sky. Then he spots the dark, falcon-shape of a jaeger as it plummets over the side of the esker toward the water. "Who scared you up?" Ozzie mutters. The red-throated loon wakes and tips its beak up toward the jaeger with perhaps the same question in mind.

The answer comes a few seconds later. Triple Seven and her two cubs waddle into view on top of the esker. They stop just above the loose sand that slopes into the lake.

"Well, look who's come for a visit," Ozzie whispers. "The notorious three bears." Ever so slowly, he sits down in his lawn chair and peers through the telescope. Just five hundred yards away, the bears are completely unaware of Ozzie's presence. They are, as Vicky would say, as *au naturel* as grizzly bears get.

The mother bear stands on her hind legs, swings her head one way, tilts her head up and sniffs, then does the same the other way. Four times she does this. Both cubs then stand and do exactly as she did—swing, tilt, sniff, four times. Their mother looks on with a seeming eye of approval. Ozzie chuckles. "You little puppets," he whispers. Then all three collapse in a heap of fur.

Ozzie adjusts the focus knob on his scope. The mother is on her back lazily scratching her stomach. The smaller cub jumps to its feet and leaps onto her throat. The other attacks her ears. Their mother rolls slowly onto her stomach, partially pinning the smaller cub, who squalls and flails beneath her. The other cub jumps on her back and buries its jaws in the patch of dark fur covering her great hump.

This roughhousing goes on until the free cub comes into range of its mother's forepaw, which she brings down on the cub's back, pinning it also. Both cubs wiggle helplessly for a while until their mother ends the game with a loud woof. They all sit up on the lip of the esker as if simply enjoying the view of the lake.

Ozzie can barely believe his eyes when he sees Triple Seven's next move. She shoves the cubs aside, then jumps over the edge.

Ozzie stifles a huge laugh as he watches her slither down the wall of sand, bum first, with her legs in the air. She hits the lake with a colossal splash. Then, with no effort at all, she climbs out and trots up the steep slope. Her cubs jump all over her and lick her wet fur. She gives them a sidelong glance, then leaps over the edge again. Ozzie almost pees his pants.

Half afloat, she hangs her front paws on the sand and grunts loudly to her cubs. They look at each other as if to say, "You first," then both tumble over the edge. They roll more than slide down the sand and land with a splash on either side of their mother.

To Ozzie, the cubs seem remarkably at home in deep water for their age. He watches them playfully batting each other while apparently treading water with their hind legs. When their mother climbs out, both cubs make a beeline for her back. She shakes them off like so much water and forges up-slope. "No free rides for you guys," says Ozzie.

After a bit more practice all of them slide down together like a family of trained gymnasts.

This is more than a treat for Ozzie. It's like the bears are onstage performing just for him. "Poor Vicky," he says, now talking right out loud as if the bears had accepted his presence. "She would'a loved this."

Ozzie takes no notes. He can record his observations later if anybody cares to ask. For now, he just watches the show. While staying dead still and keeping his emergency marshmallow supply tightly sealed in his pack, Ozzie can watch these bears simply being bears, for as long as he likes—or at least until the chopper comes.

Which it does all too soon.

CHAPTER 16

ROUNDUP

Capturing a family group can be a challenge, especially when the
cubs are only a few months old.
—*Dean Cluff*, Bear Tracks

Ralph Gloss's private jet arrives at Saber Mine ahead of schedule,
giving Benji and his father a free afternoon together. Naturally
Benji heads straight for the helipad. His timing is good. Another
bear hunt is about to begin.

When they drive up, Vicky is so busy checking equipment and
loading Siku's helicopter, she hardly looks at them. Benji detects a
definite frown on her face when she finally shakes his father's hand.

"Welcome back, Mr. Gloss."

"Catch any bears lately?" he asks.

"In fact we're just taking off to re-collar a bear at Bliss Lake."

"*Re*-collar? You lost the first one? Do you know how much
those . . ."

"Don't worry, sir. We recovered the collar. We're putting on a
new, improved model. Far more cost-effective." Vicky glances at
her watch. "I'll explain later. We must launch immediately. Are you
coming? We've got two choppers, so there's lots of room."

"Let's go, Dad," pleads Benji. "Here's your big chance to see how they spend your money."

His father shakes his head and is about to say something when the red geology chopper starts up with a roar. Then Siku's.

"It's now or never, sir," yells Vicky, pointing to the red machine.

Benji's father shrugs and, to Benji's amazement, climbs on board.

As they lift off, Benji feels more like part of the team than just a big city joyrider. Having his father beside him in the helicopter, it dawns on Benji that, for once, it's *his* turn for a tour and Benji is among the guides.

Under Vicky's orders, Siku flies his chopper back to Bliss Lake hugging the ground like a predatory hawk stealing toward its prey. Vicky spots the geology chopper far behind, struggling to follow Siku's tortuous flight path.

"What's his problem?"

"He's more used to slinging drill rigs and sandbags," says Siku, "not chasing bears."

The magic of Ozzie's afternoon by Bliss Lake fizzles when a shrill peeping noise escapes from his vest. "Damn!" he whispers gruZy. Without lifting his eye from the telescope, he digs around through several pockets trying to find his cell phone. It rings again. And again. The bears don't hear it. They're back in the water splashing each other's faces. Ozzie finally locates the phone and whips it out so fast it slips from his fingers and crashes onto a rock. "Okay, okay!" Ozzie grabs the phone and flicks it open. "Ozzie here."

All he can hear is an ear-splitting mix of static and helicopter noise. He almost hangs up when Vicky's voice breaks through. "Ozzie, we're on our way."

"Did you get Humpty-Dumpty back together again?"

"Affirmative. Everything passed inspection. We're already airborne ten miles back. See any bears?"

"You bet. The whole family showed up at the end of the esker right on cue."

"Did you get a good look at them?"

Ozzie scratches his beard for a moment watching Triple Seven and her cubs climb up their sliding hill for the sixth time. "Oh, not bad . . . I'll brief you later."

"This is too good a chance to lose, Ozzie. You know how she can vaporize in a second. Don't let her out of your sight."

"Will do, boss. Bliss Lake signing off." Ozzie is about to click off his cell phone.

"Oh, and Ozzie. We've borrowed the geologists' chopper."

"I thought you said ours was fixed."

"It is. We're in it. The other's right behind us. One for mama. One for her cubs."

"Gotcha."

"Siku and I will take care of mama. You nab the cubs in the other machine. Everything's on board: salmon net, loaded syringes, ear tags, tattoo kit, your forty-four magnum pistol."

"Anything else, Vicky?"

"Yes. You'll find Ralph Gloss, the mine owner, in the back seat of your chopper."

Ozzie shakes his head. "What timing."

"Couldn't be worse."

"Is Benji with him?"

"Affirmative. He finally talked his dad into coming."

Ozzie chuckles. Way to go kid, he thinks. "Did you charge admission?"

"Very funny. Now pack up fast."

"Roger."

Ozzie has all his gear packed before the bears reach the top of the esker. He keeps his binos trained on them, curious to see how they will react when two helicopters come screaming over the hill behind him. Already he can hear the distant pounding of their rotors. The bears hear it, too. "Sorry folks," says Ozzie, addressing the bears, "just doing our job. It's for your own good. Honest."

The bear show ends much as it started. One big one and two little ones, standing up, wagging their heads around, sniffing the air. But this time they don't stop for a playful romp in the sun. They drop to all fours and run for their lives.

The red-throated loon launches from the lake in a patter of wings. The arctic fox Ozzie smelled earlier steps out of nowhere and trots down a caribou path right in front of him.

Ozzie folds up his lawn chair, throws on his pack and whirls around just in time to see the glistening black belly of Yankee Echo Bravo shoot over the hill behind him. It sweeps upward in a steep arc as if released from a giant slingshot.

The ambush begins. Ozzie glasses the spot where he last saw the bears. They had indeed vaporized, as if gulped by an unseen trapdoor at the top of the esker.

Siku's helicopter rapidly gains altitude. They've lost her again, Ozzie thinks. If Triple Seven was in view, they'd be on her by now.

Up and up it goes. Vicky's window is open with a gun barrel sticking out. The chopper stops climbing, hovers for a moment, then suddenly drops into a steep dive and disappears behind the esker. "Bull's-eye," says Ozzie.

He whips around again, expecting to see the red chopper zoom over the hill. Crucial minutes pass. "Where the heck . . . ?" Finally he sees it, creeping over the crest of the hill, moving like a hot air balloon caught in the doldrums. Ozzie jumps up and down, waving his arms. "Come on, boys! We got bears to catch! Over here, ya dummies!"

Siku's helicopter dodges in and out of view behind the esker. Lining up for a good shot, he thinks. He turns to the other machine. "Come on! Come on! The cubs! The cubs!"

The red helicopter sluggishly descends. Ozzie jams in a couple of ear plugs and runs to the edge of the beach. The rotor-wash tears Ozzie's lawn chair from his pack and sends it skipping across the beach into the lake. Rats, he thinks. Should'a strapped it on better. As Ozzie clamps on a headset and buckles into the front seat, he watches with dismay as his favorite wildlife viewing platform sinks to the bottom of Bliss Lake.

Ozzie looks at the pilot and clicks on his microphone. "Anybody in there?" The pilot's face is shrouded in wrap-around black plastic, like the kind worn by fighter jet pilots.

The faceless head nods.

"You got a name?" Ozzie asks.

"Stanley."

"Ozzie." He notices that Stanley's knuckles are bone-white.

"You ever chased bears before?"

"Nope. First time. Vicky said you'd help with the driving."

Ozzie huffs. "Okay Stanley, head straight for Siku. I think he's on top of Triple Seven."

"Who?"

"Mama bear. Our job is to keep an eye on her cubs. Can't let them run off when she's all drugged up."

Ozzie turns around and nods to Benji and his father. Benji's wearing a ball cap from the Great Bear Research Centre.

"Where'd ya steal the hat, Benji?"

"You gave it to me last time."

"Oh yeah." Ozzie notices his father's red tie dotted with polar bears and igloos. His chubby face definitely looks a bit green. "Like helicopters?"

Mr. Gloss shakes his head. "First time. Heh-heh. Benji's idea."

Benji smiles and shrugs.

"Okay. Better sit tight."

Vicky's urgent voice invades Ozzie's headset. "Ozzie, do you copy? What's your status?'

"We're headed your way. Where are the cubs?"

"We just darted Triple Seven. Her cubs took off down the esker. I can't get a visual. You'll have to go after them."

Ozzie thrusts his hand forward a couple times, pointing to the esker. "Boot it right down the center lane."

It's good to be back, thinks Benji, glued to his favorite bubble window. As they cruise above the esker looking for lost cubs, he notices Siku's helicopter on the ground. Vicky is walking cautiously toward something. She carries a red toolbox in one hand and a pistol in the other. Then he spots the bear. Triple Seven! An electric thrill runs up Benji's spine. But the excitement is quickly tempered with a vague sadness when he notices the bear dragging herself forward by her foreclaws. The tranquilizer has knocked out most of her muscles and all she can do is scrabble through the dirt.

"Lower!" shouts Ozzie to the faceless pilot. "We won't find them at this height."

Stanley drops the chopper a little, then slows down.

"Faster! Don't lose your speed. Those cubs can really run." Ozzie turns to Benji and his father. "Start lookin', you guys. It'll take your mind off the bumps."

Benji's father grins sheepishly and fixes his gaze straight out the window. Benji sees that he's doing it all wrong. "You've gotta sweep your eyes up and down, Dad. Like a broom."

"Okay, son."

They are far down the esker when Benji spots some disturbance in the middle of a pond on his side. He whacks Ozzie on the shoulder. "Do grizzlies swim?"

"Some do, some don't. Whadya see?"

"Something swimming on that pond back there. It was no duck."

Ozzie twirls his finger in the air. "Circle back, Stanley."

"Well, I'll be . . ." says Ozzie a moment later looking through his binoculars. "Check it out, Benji," he says, handing them over.

Benji focuses on two frightened grizzly cubs swimming round and round the pond. He surprises himself at his own spotting ability. That wasn't so hard, he thinks.

"This is perfect!" says Ozzie. "Stanley, I want you to dump me on the north side of the pond, behind those big willows. Then you turn around and herd the cubs right to me across the water."

"Herd them?"

"Call it a gentle prod. You hover near the cubs pushing them toward me. Not too close or they could get spooked and drown. Once they come on shore, I nab them in my monster fishing net. Then you put down right beside me. You got that, Stanley?"

The faceless head nods.

"Good spotting, Benji. Time to round up a couple grizz."

Benji gives Ozzie a thumbs-up with his eyes still locked on the cubs. Then he hears a voice he's not used to in a helicopter. His father's.

"Nice job, son," he says, tapping Benji's knee. "We could use eyes like yours to find more diamonds. Help pay for all this pricey bear work."

They exchange an awkward glance. "Sure, Dad," says Benji.

Stanley circles tightly over the north side of the pond looking for a place to land. The willows are thick and the ground is rolling with hummocks. "Good plan, Ozzie, but I can't put down here."

Ozzie watches the ground.

Benji spots the cubs making a beeline for the far shore. "They're getting away!"

Laid-back Ozzie clicks into high gear, talking fast. "If they reach that shore before you, Stanley, we've lost them. They might not return to mama. Try that grassy spot down there."

Stanley does a few more circles. The cubs take a few more strokes. "I don't like the looks of it," he says. "Could be mushy."

This circling and tilting does not sit well with Benji's father who fumbles around looking for a barf bag. Benji pulls his out. "Take mine, Dad—I won't need it."

"That's no chopper-sucking bog, Stanley," says Ozzie. "We gotta land!"

"I'll give it one try."

"They're almost at the far shore!" says Benji, as they touch down.

"Benji, I'll need help with my gear."

Benji had no idea this was coming. "You mean . . . well, sure."

"Stanley, I want you to circle around, then head straight for them from the far shore. Don't stop to smell the flowers."

Ozzie and Benji jump out. His father gives them a soldierlike salute. He looks relieved to be on solid ground, if only for a second.

Ozzie pulls a humungous fish net out of the cargo hatch and hands it to Benji. "Let's go bag some bears!"

"Okay, boss!"

As the helicopter lifts off, Ozzie checks that his tranquilizer syringes are loaded, then slips them into a special holster on his belt. He straps on his heavy pistol, stuffs tagging and tattooing tools into his pants, then jumps into the willows. With the net held high, Benji's right behind him feeling more like a bear hunter than ever.

At first, everything goes like clockwork. Luckily Stanley gets to the cubs before they get to the shore. For a rookie bear herder he does okay, prodding them along without spooking them too much. The cubs respond exactly as Ozzie hoped, swimming back across the pond straight to them. Ozzie's net is big enough for two cubs and the plan was to scoop them both in at once just as they reached the shore. But the smaller cub is a better swimmer and reaches the shore far ahead of the other.

"I guess it's one at a time," whispers Ozzie, pulling out a syringe. "You bag him, I'll stick him. Wait till I say."

Crouched in the willows, Benji watches the cub climb onto a flat stone and shake.

"Now!" yells Ozzie.

Benji brings the net down over the cub's head. "Bull's-eye!"

Ozzie leaps on it like a wrestler. The cub, a small male, growls and snorts and tries to gouge his little claws into the strange human forms. Ozzie has to sit on the thrashing cub while he sticks the syringe in a loose fold of skin below its neck.

Benji stares at the cub, a chocolate brown bruin as fierce as it is cute.

"Oh no," says Ozzie. "*This* could be fun."

Benji looks over to see the second cub paddling full speed away from them. Meanwhile, Stanley has abandoned them for the landing site, probably assuming everything was going according to plan.

"You'll have to sit on him," says Ozzie without taking his eyes off the fleeing cub.

"What?!"

"Just until he conks out. It won't take long. Carry him back to the chopper. Dump him in the back seat. Can you handle that?"

"Well . . . I . . ."

"Then get the heck back here and I'll herd the second one into your net. Got that?"

"But . . . what do I know about handling grizzlies?"

"Just keep your face and fingers away from those little jaws. I gotta run round and scare up the other cub."

"Uh . . . right," says Benji as he gently sits down on the squirming cub. Ozzie is up like a shot and dashes down the rocky shore without another word.

The cub soon stops thrashing. His body goes limp. Benji waits a moment longer, then carefully untangles the net and lifts the precious load into his arms. Beneath his thick wet fur, Benji feels a racing flutter against his fingers, the heartbeat of a terrified cub.

As he stumbles out of the willows toward the roaring helicopter, he sees his father's face pressed against the window, his eyes wide as saucers. Benji smiles proudly, wishing somebody would take a picture of him cradling a dripping grizzly bear. But this bear isn't getting any lighter and his arms ache.

"Open the door!" Benji yells, in a wide-mouthed way that he hopes will let his father read his lips. "O-pen-the-doooor!" he yells again, thrashing one foot around as if kicking open a door. His father continues to stare out the window. He nods vigorously but doesn't get it.

Stanley finally reaches back and opens it. Benji drops the wet cub squarely on his father's suit pants. Gloss's arms go up and his jaw goes down.

"Don't let him get away," Benji yells. Then he dashes back into the willows to help Ozzie with the second cub.

By the time Benji returns to the pond, both Ozzie and the cub have vanished. The pond is still. What the . . . ? Then he spots Ozzie crouched in the willows on the far shore. He's madly pointing to some small dark shape out on the water. With the sun in Benji's face, he can't make it out. All he sees are three little bumps breaking the surface. He squints. Those can't be . . . ears? . . . and a nose? Where did you learn *that* trick?

Benji grabs the net and eases back into the willows. Ozzie wades silently into the water. Up periscope, little guy, thinks Benji. Here comes Ozzie.

Ozzie hits the water like an Olympic swimmer. The cub shoots away from him. Benji tightens his grip on the net. Like a collie dog herding sheep, Ozzie steers the cub straight for Benji's hiding spot. Benji bursts out of the bushes just before the cub gets to shore. *Sploosh!* Down goes the net and Benji scoops the cub out of the pond.

This one is much heavier than the first and Benji struggles to keep it off the ground as it thrashes in the net like an angry jackfish.

Ozzie sloshes toward him, covered in mud, and plucks the net out of his hands. "Nice catch, Benji. Settle down there, sister," he says, sitting on the cub. He has a needle in her in seconds and she goes limp soon after.

"My turn," says Ozzie as he slides his arms under her. "Whoa!" he says after a few reeling steps. "I think I picked up some extra baggage."

"What ya got in there?" asks Benji, looking at the bulging pockets of Ozzie's field-pants.

"A few tools, some muck . . . half the pond, it feels like. You go ahead and stow the net. I'll be all right."

As soon as Benji climbs on board, he heaves the first cub off his father's lap. "Thanks, Dad." His father gives him a blank look that Benji can't read. Maybe he's in shock, he thinks. "You wanted to see some bears, right?"

"TV's safer," he says with a forced chuckle.

"Well, here comes another one," says Benji spotting Ozzie with cub in arms. He's walking funny, as if his pants were falling off. Sure enough, by the time Ozzie's beside the helicopter his pants have dropped to his knees. Like a hobbled horse, he shuffles right up to Gloss's window and bangs it with his head.

"I think he wants in, Dad."

Gloss explodes into laughter. He's laughing so hard he can't work the door handle. Benji finally wrenches it open and in comes number two. *Plunk.* Another wet bear cub on the mine owner's lap.

Soon the six of them—four humans and two grizzly bears—are flying back to Vicky, Siku, and Triple Seven.

"Good performance back there," says Stanley. "Is that unusual in your business?"

"All in a day's work," says Ozzie matter-of-factly. "Should'a done the whole routine on 'em—tagging and everything, I mean. Lost too much time at the swimming hole. The trick now is to get everybody back together before the tranquilizer wears off."

Benji checks the eyes of both cubs. He gasps when he sees them open. "They're waking up already!"

"Don't worry," says Ozzie. "They've lost all muscle control. You'll know pretty quick when they get it back."

Vicky doesn't even look up as they fly right over her head, tuck in beside Siku's chopper, and power down. She is hard at work on her favorite bear.

Ozzie scoops the female cub off Gloss's lap, plods over to Triple Seven, and sets it down on her mother's back. Without waiting for orders, Benji lugs the runt male out of the chopper and offers it to Ozzie with a wide grin.

"Oh . . . thanks, Benji." Ozzie takes the cub and carefully sets him down beside his sister. He motions Benji to come closer. "We still have a lot of work to do. You can watch, but if mama wakes up, boot it to the chopper."

While Ozzie and Vicky lose themselves in taking countless measurements, Benji steps closer to Triple Seven. He is spellbound by the panting grizzly, lying so close he can smell her barnyard bouquet. That steamy broth of fear and fascination swirls in his stomach.

Vicky has the bear belly down on a bright blue tarp with her front and back legs spread out in perfect symmetry. It strikes Benji that she looks like a great hairy skydiver sailing down through the air. The summer sun has bleached the bear's fur to a golden blonde. Her massive paws are chestnut brown—like she's wearing boxing gloves—as is her great hump which heaves up and down with each pant.

Benji moves around to look into Triple Seven's face. There's a long, deep scar across her muzzle. Wow, he thinks. Who gave you *that?* He leans closer to examine it. Her drugged eyes follow him. They stare unblinking into his.

In those bottomless eyes he sees a fierce green fire that no tranquilizer can touch. He sees a proud strength unmoved by temporary defeat, a strength that carries her through life's cruelties—like the brutal death of her cub. Then he sees a reflection of himself.

A weak, raspy growl escapes from the bear's huffing mouth. Benji pulls back.

Vicky looks up from her work. "Isn't she magnificent?"

Benji can only nod, speechless.

"Vic," says Ozzie, sounding alarmed. "Her collar."

"Don't worry about the tranquilizer. There's plenty of time. We've got lots of data to gather."

Benji watches Vicky working feverishly as she measures Triple Seven's claws, paws, and body length. She fires the numbers to

Ozzie who records them in her field book. She measures fat levels, takes several blood samples, even checks for tooth decay.

Finally, Vicky sits up and sighs. Benji thinks she's finished.

"Of course I'll need a scat sample," she says, addressing Triple Seven's face. "Come on, Mama, we drugged you almost an hour ago. Can't you produce for me, *please?*" Vicky starts slipping on rubber gloves. "Okay, I guess I'll just have to help myself . . ."

"Gross!" says Benji who has just figured out what Vicky is about to do.

"Forget the scats, Vic," says Ozzie. "We need to get that collar on. Don't you have one of those new-fangled models rigged up for her?"

"Yes, of course. It's in the back of Siku's machine." As Ozzie gets up Vicky notices his mud-caked pants. "Where in the world were you?"

"Later, Vic. I still have to tag and measure the cubs. How much time left for Mom?"

Vicky looks at her watch. "Twenty minutes at least."

Benji crouches to look again into Triple Seven's eyes. That fire behind them seems brighter. "Are you *sure* she's still stoned?"

Vicky sticks her hand in the bear's drooling mouth. "Would I do this if she wasn't?"

Ozzie runs back with a blue plastic collar. Three red 7's are painted on the side. "Pretty fancy. Radio, satellite, and GPS transmitters all on board?"

"Nothing but the best for our bears. And look at this." Vicky slips the collar over the bear's head, snaps it closed, then looks at Ozzie with a rare twinkle in her eye.

Ozzie studies the new collar for a moment. "Wait a minute. Where's the breakaway piece? How does this thing ever fall off?"

"The old breakaway collars are too unreliable. They're supposed to last three years then drop, but you never know for sure. Look what happened to hers. This is a *blowaway* collar. There's a tiny electronic detonator in the collar's connector. When—and *only* when—I give the signal from my new telemetry box, the detonator blows and the collar drops."

Ozzie shakes his head. "What'll they think of next?"

Benji whistles. "Sweet." He realizes that, in the world of high tech biology, this woman is a master.

"Watch this." Vicky pulls the telemetry box out of her pack. She reaches for a shiny red key hanging around her neck. She flips open a special cover on the telemetry panel marked *collar release,* inserts the key, and turns it. Ozzie hears a faint electronic click, and the collar springs open.

"You see," says Vicky proudly. "This technology allows me to automatically pop this thing off at precisely the moment I choose."

"Cool," says Benji.

"Sounds right up your alley, Vic," says Ozzie. "Leave nothing to chance . . ."

As if on cue, the big bear lifts its great head and roars.

Benji gasps. "Is that supposed to happen?"

"Quick!" cries Vicky. "Get that thing closed! The tranquilizer's wearing off way too soon."

Ozzie wraps his arms around the bear's throat and clicks the collar shut. "What dose did you give her?"

"The same as last August when we first collared her. I can tell you precisely." Vicky thumbs through her field book while Ozzie hastily loads another syringe.

Benji backs away on legs that suddenly feel like rubber. The bear lies between him and the helicopters.

"Ah, here it is," says Vicky. "I gave her . . ."

Before she can even read the numbers to Ozzie, Triple Seven boosts herself up on her forelegs, whips her head around and knocks Ozzie flat on his back as if he were a paper doll.

"Mother!" says Benji.

Triple Seven gives Benji a dirty look while struggling to get up on all fours. Her limp cubs fall off like potato sacks. Then, slowly, on semi-paralyzed legs, she trudges toward Vicky, who is backing toward the helicopters.

"Nice bear. Good bear," she says in low tones that are supposed to sound friendly but are trembly with fear.

Triple Seven stumbles into Vicky's toolbox, spilling its contents with a loud crash. She angrily chomps on it, gives it a few wild shakes, then hurls it into the bushes like a useless bone.

The bear advances on her, tossing its head back and making hollow popping noises with its jaws.

"Nice bear. We don't mean any harm. Nice . . ." Vicky trips on a clump of cottongrass and falls backward. The bear lunges for her.

Ozzie is back on his feet. "Get behind me, Benji!" he yells as he draws his pistol. Benji leaps over to him, his eyes fixed on the stalking bear. He knows that with one good shot Ozzie could, if he had to, send a bullet cleanly into Triple Seven's brain. Then he realizes that with one bad shot Ozzie could send the same bullet into Vicky, one of the choppers, or his father, who is buckled inside safe and sound, though looking greener than ever.

"Don't shoot, Ozzie!" says Benji in a quavering voice.

Ozzie shoots. Into the air. *BOOM!* The bear lifts its head long enough for Vicky to deliver a steel-toed boot to the bear's chin and scramble to her feet. Ozzie fires another shot. *BOOM!* The bear halts on wobbly legs.

Siku blasts his siren and starts his engine. Stanley gets the idea and does the same.

Benji throws in his two bits. "Nice bear. Go away, bear!"

Vicky is a few steps from Siku's helicopter when she trips again. Benji can't believe what he sees next. Amid the deafening riot of helicopter noise, Triple Seven continues to advance. This time she clamps down on her boot and begins shaking it like she did her toolbox. *BOOM!* Unfazed, the bear continues shaking her boot.

"Stay behind me!" yells Ozzie as he sneaks around for a cleaner shot at the bear.

Over Ozzie's shoulder, Benji watches in horror as Vicky, still on her back, delivers futile kicks to Triple Seven's head with her free boot. It looks like she's trying to untangle something from around her neck. "What's she *doing?*"

"Dunno," says Ozzie, raising his pistol.

The bear lifts its head for a moment and bellows at the shrieking helicopters. Benji notices his father frantically trying to find the lock on his door.

Vicky unsnarls her oversize binoculars and starts swinging them above her head.

"She's gonna bonk it!" exclaims Benji.

"Here bear," yells Vicky. "Chew on *this!*" And with her binos, she gives her favorite bear a swift, solid bop on the nose.

It works. Triple Seven pushes off from her leg and whirls around in retreat. The bear's muscles are her own again, and she gallops toward the lake with astounding speed. Benji feels his heart drop back from his throat.

Ozzie holsters his gun and shouts at Benji to help him gather the scattered tools and tarp. Running back to the helicopter, they stop to check on the cubs. Both of them still look pretty dopey. Ozzie tries to flip the male cub onto its belly but is met with jaws snapping close to his face. The other cub tries to slash Benji's legs with her claws. He jumps out of range just in time.

"Too late for tagging or tattooing these guys," Ozzie yells. "Let's get outta here."

Stanley's helicopter is first to lift off. He seems in an awful hurry to get back to camp.

"We'll make you a bear pilot yet," says Ozzie.

"Thanks anyway," says Stanley, "but I think I'll stick to slinging sand."

"Can't hack it, eh?" says Gloss, rapping Benji's shoulder. "Talk to my son here. Seems like he could give you a few pointers about handling wild grizzlies."

Benji flashes a grin at his dad, then turns back to the window. He watches Triple Seven bounding toward the lake. Every few paces she stops to scratch her new collar. Benji tries to remember the name Ozzie gives to those collars. What was it? Oh yeah. Electronic leash. He wonders how long she'll have to wear it before she's free again.

"Good thing your bear didn't stand up beside the helicopter," says Siku once they, too, are up and away. "Mighta got its head chopped off."

"We haven't seen the last of her," says Vicky rubbing her sore foot. "There's a lot of data we didn't get down there. Her cubs aren't even tagged, for gosh sakes. But at least we got that new collar on. That thing's not coming off till I say so."

"Whatever you say, boss," says Siku as he steers his black and yellow bird for Saber Mine.

FALL

CHAPTER 17

GUARD DOWN

In one instance, a lone caribou calf was observed approximately twenty meters directly downwind of an adult female with two cubs of the year.

The female and her cubs were aware of the calf's presence but they appeared more intent to feed on berries.

—Rob Gau, Bear Tracks

September 15.

The boundless land all around the big bear now boils with color. Since the sopping rains of August, it's as if the landscape has spun a misty cocoon and emerged totally transformed. Rivers of red and copper ooze like blood around cells of gray bedrock. Rimming every pond and lake is a halo of gold and yellow willows. A dazzling blanket of orange and green mosses accents the lower ground. Slicing through this colorful quilt are ribbons of shining sand. The sky is a perfect dome of brittle blue, full of snap and brilliance. The bear crouches and makes a great turd that steams in the morning chill.

High above her comes the rush and rustle of wings as flock after flock of birds fly south—the gulls and geese, the shorebirds and sparrows, even the Lapland longspurs, whose timeless, tinkling courtship songs seemed to anchor them forever to this land and no other. But they retreat with the rest to the Mississippi grainfields and coastal lagoons. For the most part, none but the ravens remain. And two of them now circle slowly over the bear, waiting for something to die.

Let the birds fly away. Let the caribou make a run for the treeline. This bear won't budge. She remains rooted to a land now bursting with berries. She stuffs herself with berries, feeding all day and through most of the star-filled night. This morning's menu is mostly crowberries and bearberries, which the cubs, too, are beginning to enjoy between bouts of boisterous play.

The mother bear lies spread-eagled in the berry patch. Using claws that have smashed the necks of caribou and sent boulders flying across the tundra, she delicately plucks the berries one by one. Other times she swings her head from side to side and uses her flexible, monkeylike lips to strip the fruit from one branch after another. Her nose is never still, always twisting and turning, making her face screw up like a wrinkly old woman who just swallowed a lemon.

She strips all the branches within reach, then wiggles forward on her belly, cutting out a new swath through the patch. Hour after berry-filled hour she gorges like this, laying on a thick winter overcoat of fat. Sometimes she raises her purple snout into the crisp autumn air to tease out any new odors. But mostly she stuffs herself, concentrating on nothing but berries, berries, and more berries.

At one point the ravens, still circling over the bear, come so teasingly close she rears up and takes a swipe at them. Another time, a stray caribou calf, completely alone and defenseless, appears over a small knoll within lunging distance of the bear. She does no more than lift her nose and sniff, without even looking at it, then goes back eating.

Later in the afternoon, as the weakening sun slides toward the horizon, a young female grizzly and her brother show up on the other side of a deep pond near where the big bear is feeding. At the smell of them, her cubs jump on her back and try to hide behind her massive shoulder hump. She reaches around and bats them off. As for the visiting bears, she gives them a dirty look, a quick grunt, then ignores them, too. There are enough berries to go around.

The cubs relax, eventually falling off their mother and into sleep. The two grizzly strangers graze on berries for a while, then disappear. The mother bear eats and eats, stuffing in thousands of berries every hour. A full moon rises. The first stars come out. She eats more.

Only one scent can distract her. Her worst enemy. The giant male who killed her cub.

As if snapping out of a daze, the mother bear suddenly sits up on her haunches and sniffs the cold, damp air. There is no wind to bring her new messages. But something in the air makes her eyes dart, her heart race. She hears nothing except the faraway rush of water and the faint peeping of migrating sandpipers overhead. She can see well enough. The western sky is still awash with orange and purple hues which cast a ghostly light over an already glowing landscape. All is still. Yet a long, rumbling growl rises from somewhere deep in her throat.

Like an alarm bell, the sound wakes her cubs. They are hungry and want no more berries. They want to nurse. She reluctantly leans back and lets them climb aboard, all the while keeping her head high and pivoting around. But before the cubs can latch on, she is up again, this time on her hind feet, sniffing hard.

Then, from behind her, she hears a new sound, that raspy click of long bear claws scratching over ice-worn bedrock. She whirls around. Her whole body stiffens. In the swelling moonlight she can just make out the shape of a large grizzly lumbering along the shore of the pond just below her. She can't smell him and, judging by the bear's moseying pace, he can't smell her either. In the dead calm of evening only the scent of berries fills her nose.

She looks for her cubs. They're gone. She drops down to sniff out their scent and picks up a trail leading to a patch of dense willows next to the pond. The willows shake. The cubs must be in there chasing a vole or something. She cautiously turns to the intruding bear. It's his turn to stand. He's trying to make sense of the commotion in the bushes blocking his path. The mother bear still can't smell him, but his profile against the moonlit water is unmistakable—that drooping lower lip, that torn ear, that mammoth hulk of a body, now looking all the larger with a potbelly stretched wide with berries.

She freezes. Only her eyes move, shifting from the shaking willows to the standing bear and back again. In seconds he could be upon them, and her cubs would be torn to pieces.

She slinks to a crouch, then waits till he drops to all fours. In two bounds, she leaps onto his back. The giant male lets out a surprised, howling roar. She sinks her teeth into his thick neck before he springs to a stand and she is thrown backward into the stony shallows. She crash-lands on her back. For an awful second, he looks down on her as if from a high cliff. Her nose squirms as it fills with that terrible odor of sour musk. Then, with a dead weight almost twice her own, he falls on her with open jaws and raking claws.

Pieces of fur fly into the water, some of it his, most of it hers. He rips open her shoulder and slices at her face. Then she clamps down hard on his nose only to be knocked almost senseless by a mighty blow to her head. The force throws her out into deeper water. He hesitates for a moment, then falls on her again. This time he gives her throat a crushing bite that would have killed her instantly had his teeth not struck her bulky satellite collar. He recoils with an insulted snort, giving her just enough time to squirm out from under him. He lunges for her, wrapping his forelegs around her waist. But he can't get a good grip on her wet fur, and she flees.

She runs straight for the willows where her terrified cubs have been watching the fight. When they see her bounding toward them, they run into the open and try to climb on her back.

But this is no time for piggybacks. The attacking grizzly, though stumbling on the slippery rocks, is almost within striking range. Any escape is blocked by the willows and, farther down the shore, a row of house-sized boulders. While her cubs frantically scratch and paw at her side, she casts a desperate glance down the shore from where her attacker had come. The route is clear, but her cubs could never outrun him.

There's only one thing to do. She spanks them back into the willows, then stands to face her attacker head-on. He dodges her, lunging instead for her retreating cubs. She charges after him, and just as the cubs disappear into the willows, she fiercely slashes his rear end with her claws.

This is not the kind of challenge he can ignore. Forgetting the cubs for the moment, he whirls around and again knocks the mother bear flat with one blow. She staggers to her feet just in time to swerve to one side as he charges full speed toward her. He slips on the rocks. She pounces on his back. He throws her off. She charges. Taking slash after slash, she throws herself back into battle, again and again, luring the giant male away from her cubs and out to deeper water.

As soon as the water is deep enough to swim, she struggles free and lunges toward the center of the pond. She is as much at home in water as on land. Perhaps she can tire him out with a good water chase or lead him to the far shore for yet another battle—*anything* to keep him away from her cubs.

While swimming away, she looks over her shoulder to make sure he is following. Again, the giant male hesitates. He makes a few false charges after her, then retreats to shallower water. He lunges at her several more times, roaring loudly and gnashing his teeth. Each time he refuses to wade deeper than his chest. As she makes for the opposite shore, her attacker races toward her, skirting the shallows and kicking up huge walls of spray that glitter in the moonlight. She turns and tries to swim back the way she came. He splashes round to meet her. She turns again. So does he. Back and forth she goes across the pond. Round and round he goes along its edge.

Finally, the mother bear stops luring him and merely treads water at the center of the deep pond. She is trapped here, but safe. As for her cubs, they are nowhere in sight.

It seems this big scary bear is deathly afraid of deep water. Nobody had ever taught him how to swim.

Unable or unwilling to pursue her, he flies into a rage, bellowing louder than before. For a while he crashes back and forth through the shallows, kicking up spray and charging the floating bear as far into the water as he dares. She watches the whole show while calmly treading water. Every time he seems to lose interest in her, she moves in closer, taunting him with occasional splashes of her paw. She must wait it out. She must distract him.

But suddenly, after letting off more than a trainload of steam, the huge male turns his back on her, heads straight for the shore, and attacks the clump of willows where the cubs had been hiding. He thrashes them furiously. He tugs and tugs on one bush until it finally lets go, roots and all, and he falls back into the pond bum first. With the bush still in his jaws, he does his best to shake the life out of it, then hurls it at the floating bear.

Suddenly, as if she never existed, he crashes back into the clump of willows and out the other side.

Under the pale moonlight, the mother bear watches him trot purposefully up and over the berry-crammed hill. He doesn't look back. He doesn't stop even for a nibble. He keeps his nose close to the ground.

The mother bear knows he's found the scent trail of her cubs.

CHAPTER 18

IN CAMP

Sometimes, when they're really scared, they may go to more marginal habitats where aggressive males usually won't follow. They may even move toward human structures. That opens up a whole host of new problems.
—*Vivian Banci, Bear Biologist*

All her instincts rebel with each painful step toward the southwest. Yet there is no denying that her cubs went this way—straight for the mining camp. And the giant male, too, undoubtedly following the same scent trail as she. The moon casts a waxy sheen on the landscape, enough light to see faint colors in the glowing tundra shrubs. But she could follow this trail with her eyes closed, so thick and so fresh is the scent of grizzly.

The underscent of humans already prickles her nose. Burnt plastic and oil, exhaust fumes, and paint. She snorts in disgust, but veers neither left nor right from the trail set by her cubs. With her right shoulder slashed almost to the bone and a forepaw ripped wide open, the best she can do is a jerky limp.

She has been trudging forward for over an hour, and now, up ahead, she sees a gush of glaring light that drowns out the moon and stars. It streams upward from a place where, to her knowledge, the sun never rises or sets. It's the miners, digging up diamonds throughout the tranquil arctic night.

She limps along, dreading each step, repelled by the mine and the stench of the giant male, yet drawn by her devotion to her cubs. She doesn't stop to lick her wounds, quench her thirst, or even gulp down a few berries. She slows her determined pace only when a sudden mine explosion deep underground momentarily turns the rock-solid tundra to jelly. As the shock waves enter her paws, she raises them high off the ground and shakes them one by one, as if she had just stepped on hot coals.

Farther along, she breaks her stride and stands to see where the scent trail is taking her. It leads directly to the lights. They flood from a gigantic hole in the ground. She drops down and shakes her head as if scattering flies. She is confused. Her memory tells her there should be a small lake at that spot, a lake where, years ago, she and her mother had feasted on eggs robbed from the nests of white-fronted geese. She limps farther down the scent trail, closer to the lights. A steady drone of machine noise turns into a roar.

The bear stops abruptly at a cliff edge that was once a shoreline. The lake she knew is now a colossal open pit. Clouds of dust, tinted orange by floodlights, billow upward, as if escaping from the mouth of a volcano. She leans forward to peer into the pit. Through the dust she can make out a monstrous yellow machine clawing at the ground, scooping out fields of boulders and shattered bedrock with each swipe. The thing spins around and dumps its load into other yellow machines, half as big, that have round black feet three times the height of a human and two small eyes that throw a piercing white light.

The cubs' scent trail ends smack on this spot. Did they fall in? She crouches and tips her head over the bedrock wall but sees no brown furry lumps at the bottom. She probes the dust and blasted rock with her nose. The shattered fragments along the edge of the pit dig into her wounded paw, and she winces in pain between each frantic sniff.

Then, through her dust-clogged nose, she picks up a hint of cub scent and follows it around the pit's edge. It leads to a wide gravel trail rising out of the pit. Here she loses the scent completely. In spite of the pain, she runs back and forth along the edge of the road, unwilling to give up the search, unsure about crossing. The moment she gets up the nerve to cross, the road floods with white light as a loaded haul truck emerges from the pit. Without hesitation, the bear stands up in the middle of the road. This beast will not get her cubs.

Through the swirling dust, the driver spots the shining blonde bear in her headlights just in time. She stops her truck so fast that a large chunk of diamond-bearing kimberlite ore spills over the top of her box, crashes down to the road and rolls almost to the bear's feet. The bear pounces on the rock and, with one powerful sweep of her uninjured forepaw, hurls it off into the night. She stands again and holds her ground. The driver honks a train-sized horn. The bear doesn't budge. The driver tries flashing her headlights on and off. The bear raises her claws and roars. It's a standoff between a monster truck and an angry mother bear. Another haul truck comes grinding up the hill, almost crashing into the first. Then, with a final defiant roar, the bear drops to all fours and lumbers down the other side of the road without giving the giant trucks another glance.

After some determined snuffling along the boulder-strewn road-bank, she picks up the scent trail once again. Here the comforting odor of her cubs is almost overwhelmed by the sour stink of the belligerent male. He must have been almost right on top of them here, paw for paw. His scent is so strong the mother bear stands and peers ahead, expecting to see his form against the harsh orange lights of the mining camp.

Ignoring the lights, the pain, and the thickening scent of humans, she runs toward the camp, keeping her nose glued to the ground. *Crash!* Something thin and metallic stings her forehead, and a split second later, she is thrown backward by a mighty surge of energy that strangles every muscle of her body. Sprawled on her back, she retches a couple times, then rolls onto her feet and shakes off the spasm.

She growls at this new enemy, the electric bear fence just doing its job. At close range it is virtually invisible to her. Still growling under her breath, she slowly stalks forward, again following the cubs' scent trail . . . *Zap!* She gets hit with another ten thousand volts. Once she collects herself, she stands this time to get a better look at what exactly is attacking her. Though it is too dark to see the wires, she spots the snippets of flagging tape tied here and there along them.

For a third time she approaches the fence but stops just before it to closely inspect the scent trail. The smell of both cubs goes right up to the wire. Here it is smothered by the smell of urine from the adult male. She sniffs first to one side, then the other. There is a faint odor of fox, a whiff of ptarmigan, but no grizzly. Cautiously, she inches her nose through the bottom two wires. The cub trail continues. The adult male's does not. Shock or no shock, while fleeing from their attacker, the little cubs must have squeezed right through the fence. Now they are somewhere inside the mining camp. But where is the giant male?

She backtracks a little along the scent trail, trying to determine where he went. Foiled by the fence, maybe he finally gave up the chase and took off the way he came. That might explain why his scent is so strong close to camp. But wouldn't she have bumped into him on the way out?

She backtracks some more, finding no clues to the mystery. Then something powerful tugs on her heart. Forget the big male. Rescue the cubs.

The mother bear returns to the fence and starts prowling along it, looking for a way in. A wide stretch of gravel lies between her and a long row of red trailers. It's the runway. Just as she nears one end of it, a set of blazing floodlights goes on. The bear draws back in terror at what she sees—two shiny helicopters, one red, one black.

At the sight of them, she automatically runs for cover behind a big rock. Her pulse quickens when she hears human mouth sounds approaching. Two humans carrying metal boxes walk toward the helicopters. She narrows her eyes against the glare of the lights and studies the strange two-legged creatures. They climb all over the machines without ever getting inside. There is no deafening engine noise. No sickening fumes or belching smoke. Both helicopters lie still. They must be sleeping. The bear can safely escape. She crouches down and creeps catlike out of range of the floodlights toward the other side of camp, which lies in shadow.

That sharp rankness and sweat smell of humans grows stronger as she sneaks behind the camp. The scent makes her hackles rise.

But she knows her cubs are in there somewhere, so she continues following the fence, looking for some kind of weak spot or opening. At last she finds one. Somebody forgot to latch a truck gate, and it hangs open by a crack. After a couple of nasty shocks, she figures out how to swing it open, then dashes through. She wanders into the heart of the mining camp and is soon surrounded by trailers and trucks.

There are no humans about. They must be burrowed inside. The ones working on the helicopters will block her path so she can't go back to the runway to pick up the cubs' scent. She must call them. She starts with a low motherly woof. A ground squirrel darts out from under one of the trailers into the moonlight. It stares at her, then ducks under a building that has particularly sweet smells leaking from it. The cook shack. Memories of an apple core she once ate distract the bear for a moment and she starts to drool. Then she remembers the fiery spray in her mouth and the blinding pain in her eyes right after she ate it, and she is tempted no more.

She stands and woofs again, a little louder. This time she gets a response. Over the dull throb of generator noise, she hears a long low grunt coming from near the gate where she came in.

It's not the cubs. It's him. The giant male. He's followed her right into camp.

She shudders at the sight of his tall silhouette looming black against the moonlight. Splinters of light spilling from camp illuminate his long claws and broken teeth. The two bears stare and sniff at each other through the darkness—her, hemmed in by a ring of trailers and shacks, and him, the silent night stalker, ready to attack at any moment.

Weakened by hunger, thirst, and crippling wounds, the mother bear now faces her bitterest foe. Fear fills her veins where strength and courage once flowed. Then she remembers her cubs. She straightens herself and lets go a valiant roar.

The giant male simply sniffs with greater gusto. At close range, the camp is overflowing with rich odors that seem much to his liking. She drops down and fakes a charge. He sponges up smells without even looking at her. She roars again, getting a response she had hoped for earlier but which now could spell disaster.

From the pitch-dark crawl space under the trailers comes the familiar squeal of her runt cub. The giant adult male hears it, too, and instantly storms toward the sound. The mother bear lunges into his path with bared fangs and brandished claws. He bowls her over with ease and dives under the building like a ground squirrel down a hole. As he goes in, both cubs shoot right past him, fleeing their hiding place for the protection of their long lost mother. Before they can duck behind her, the giant male scrambles back out and charges the lot of them.

A flash of light and a screeching burst of human mouth sounds stop him in his tracks. The mother bear wheels around just in time to see a human dodge back into the cook shack and slam the door. As if a temporary truce had been called, all four bears, including the cubs, stand side by side, watching the door to see what will happen next. They hear more excited mouth sounds and thumping noises from inside.

The smells released from the open door are working their magic on the giant male. It's breakfast time for the nightshift miners and bacon and eggs are being served. The mother bear recoils at the smell of human food—not wanting another blast of fire in her face—and she and her cubs slowly back away. But the giant male is gripped by these odors which he connects with tasty rewards from other tundra camps that he has visited—and often trashed. Tonight is his third raid on this camp alone.

The bear family fades back, inching closer to the open truck gate. The giant male meanwhile creeps ahead, toward the promise of scrumptious human goodies. After another burst of mouth sounds from inside, the cook shack door suddenly flies open and a big hairy human steps out. He is carrying a long metal object that he points into the darkness. Another smaller human rushes to his side and wildly waves a blinding light back and forth across the gravel until it comes to rest on the giant male.

The mother bear seizes this chance to make a run for it, and she and her cubs sprint through the open gate. Just as they veer off the road and out onto the moon-washed tundra, they hear the frightening crack of a shotgun echoing off the boulders all around them.

CHAPTER 19

DEAD END

You're chasing the bear, you're chasing the bear, you're chasing
    the bear, then you give up.
—*Anonymous,* C'est La Vie

"Three strikes and you're out, Buster Bear," says Siku.

Vicky and Ozzie crouch beside the dead bear, trying to shove a
rope net under his huge bloody mass.

"Siku, make yourself useful and help get this net under," says
Vicky. "I want to weigh him before skinning him out."

"What do you think lured him in last night?" asks Ozzie
between grunts.

Vicky looks over at the camp trailers. "Beats me. This is the
cleanest mine north of sixty. High tech bear fence, super-efficient
garbage incinerator, no hunting, no fishing. There's nothing here
for bears. They just fired a guy for pitching an orange peel out of
his truck."

"I heard somebody left a gate open," says Siku.

"Somebody goofed all right. But what lured him in? It wasn't
like last time. That cook was asking for it by storing bacon grease
behind the cook shack."

"They fired her, too, didn't they?" asks Ozzie.

"Of course. Siku, yank on that rope. The net's almost through."

They finally wrap the net around Buster. Vicky hooks an electronic scale to its top rope. "We're ready, Siku. Get the chopper."

As Ozzie wipes the blood off his hands with a rag, he looks at Vicky sideways. "Somebody heard lots of roaring last night, as if a couple bears were wrestling outside. Do you think it was . . . ?"

Vicky almost jumps on him. "Impossible! When I checked Triple Seven's position late yesterday she was miles away, not moving at all."

"Probably feasting on a good berry patch."

"I can understand Buster skipping right into camp, but Triple Seven? One whiff of humans and she's off like a race horse."

"Thanks to biologists like us," says Ozzie with a faint smirk. He perks one ear to the sky then squints at something off to the southeast. "Here comes the Herc."

Out of a lumpy patch of bear-shaped clouds flies one of the fattest, brawniest, and loudest planes flying the northern skies—a Super Hercules. Aimed straight for the mine, the plane remains a speck that seems to hover motionless in the clouds. Only the rising thunder from its motors says it's getting closer.

Through his binoculars Ozzie makes out the plane's black snub nose and distinctive red-and-white paint job. "I heard it was loaded with TVs."

"And three soft ice-cream machines," says Vicky. "Gotta keep those miners happy."

As the hundred-foot plane touches down, its huge propellers kick up a sky-high cloud of choking dust. Ozzie watches the back ramp of the plane drop open like the gaping mouth of an enormous bird. The first thing to come down the ramp is not a bull-dozer or pickup truck. Not even an ice-cream machine. It's Benji with a video camera glued to his nose.

Ozzie taps Vicky lightly on the shoulder. "Oh . . . I, ah . . . forgot to tell you. The camp manager phoned yesterday. Says Benji's working on some kind of science project. He wanted to do something on grizzly bears so his dad sent him back up here."

"Alone?"

"Yep."

"For a science project?"

"Yep."

"But the kid lives in San Francisco."

"Remember what they're mining down there, Vicky. Diamonds. This guy's loaded. Gloss flew him up to Winnipeg in his private jet. You know how Benji loves aircraft. So they let him hop on the Herc."

Vicky frowns. "So why doesn't he do his project on airplanes?"

"Have you read his e-mails lately? He's more nuts on bears than even you."

Vicky glances over at the dead grizzly. "His timing couldn't be worse!"

"No," says Ozzie thoughtfully. "He needs to see this."

Benji continues slowly down the long ramp, now walking backward with his video camera pointed into the open belly of the plane. A puff of blue smoke escapes and a forklift truck appears, dwarfed by a huge truck tire in its claws. Benji films the load going down the ramp, then swings his camera around to Ozzie and Vicky. While still filming, he takes off his pilot's cap and waves it above his head.

Ozzie takes off his Saber Mines cap and does the same. "He wants us to smile," he says through his teeth.

Vicky nods her head and gives Benji a limp grin. "This is ridiculous!" she mutters.

"Careful, Vicky," he says, still smiling and waving his hat. "You're on camera. Remember Project Benji? Show him a good time or his dad might stop pumping diamond money into your bear work."

Benji, still filming, is about to step off the ramp—into thin air—when the forklift operator, who happened to look up at him, honks his horn. Benji catches himself just in time, and comes running over to meet the bear crew.

"Hey, bear huggers. Did you see me tip our wings?"

Ozzie shakes his hand. "They let you fly *that?*

"Skipper gave me his hat, too." Benji takes off the star-studded cap and admires it. "Collector's item. I'll hang it beside that bear hat you gave—" As he plunks it back on, he sees the bear. "Is that . . . *Buster?*"

"Uh-huh," says Vicky quietly.

"So you finally managed to dart him?" Benji whips out his video camera and starts walking toward him.

"Well, not exactly," she says. "You see, Benji . . ."

Benji hears no more. At that moment Siku, who has been warming up his helicopter, lifts off and starts flying toward the bear. Benji rolls his camera. He films Vicky running over to hook the net to the helicopter's sling. Vicky gives Siku two thumbs up. They better dump him far from camp before he wakes up, thinks Benji. Then he wonders why they'd bring him into camp in the first place. As the bear leaves the ground, the net squeezes around its limp body and something starts dripping from it. Benji zooms in on fresh trickles of blood. Ouch. Buster, are you okay? The bear's head flops down at an odd angle revealing a gaping red wound on its neck.

Benji suddenly lowers his camera with his finger still glued to the record button—capturing a close-up of his left hiking boot and the shriek of helicopter noise. Benji remembers Buster running from the chopper during that first flight in May. Buster, the towering monster whose flashing claws nearly tore Benji's heart out, stirring up strange memories of stone claws, his mother's scream, falling into darkness. . . . Those terrible claws, now held in a death pose over the great bear's chest. As scary as Buster was, Benji now feels like weeping.

A big hand taps his shoulder. It's Ozzie trying to lead him away from the noise.

"What happened?" asks Benji as they duck behind a pickup.

"Remember that saying: a fed bear is a dead bear?"

Benji nods. "So who fed him?"

"Can't say. Once upon a time Buster stuck his nose where he shouldn't have and got hooked on human food. Who knows where he first tasted it? An open garbage pit five hundred miles away. Maybe some sloppy campers."

"What about this place?"

"Your dad runs a squeaky clean camp. But for bears like Buster, the mere whiff of humans means food. Once they get that idea stuck in their heads they're as good as dead. You dump a bunch of diamond-hungry humans on Buster's turf and . . . well, look what happens."

Benji fingers the diamond stud in his eyebrow. It had all seemed like a game. Just another rip-roaring arctic adventure. And now, the first grizzly bear Benji had ever seen was dead. Shot through the neck with a lead slug. An anger he'd never felt before boils up and he turns to Ozzie with narrowed eyes. *"You* killed him, didn't you."

"Technically, yes."

"What do you mean, *technically?"*

"I was the one who pulled the trigger . . ."

"Are you saying my *dad* killed him? Putting a mine here?"

"No, Benji, I . . ."

"He pays you big bucks to protect grizzlies. Then you go and shoot 'em?"

"He also pays us to protect people."

Benji's head hurts. It doesn't make sense. "Can't you untrain bears like Buster? Teach 'em that humans mean trouble, not food."

"We tried that with the helicopter last May, remember? Works sometimes. But really it's the humans you gotta teach. All it takes is a couple of nuisance humans to create a nuisance bear that raises hell all over the tundra. They're the ones who killed Buster."

"Oh," says Benji.

"Takes more than fancy data to protect these bears."

"I guess so."

They watch in solemn silence as Siku gently lowers the dead bear to the runway.

"It boils down to one question," says Ozzie. "Can humans and grizzlies coexist out here?"

This land was once a barren wasteland for Benji. Now he knows it pulses with life. The tundra without grizzlies is as unimaginable to him as the sky without stars. "Well . . . can we?"

Ozzie shrugs. "Time will tell, Benji. Time will tell."

Once Siku moves off and powers down, Ozzie and Benji walk back to have a last look at Buster. Vicky stands over him with her nose in her field book.

"So, what's he weigh?' asks Ozzie.

"Big bruiser, all right. Seven hundred and fifty pounds. Largest tundra grizzly on record."

"What'll you do with him?" asks Benji.

Vicky looks over at Benji with raised eyebrows. "You were kinda fond of the old guy."

"Pretty gutsy grizzly. First one I'd seen."

"Tell him, Ozzie."

"Well, first we skin him out . . ."

For a second, Benji pictures Buster's hide hanging in his attic room in San Francisco, then shakes the idea from his head. "Who gets the hide?"

"You interested?" asks Ozzie.

"No way."

"Good. It's already spoken for. Native hunters."

"Like Siku's relatives?"

"Maybe."

"And the body?"

"We chop his head off. Send it to the government biologists. They yank a tooth, age it, do DNA studies, that kinda stuff."

"And the rest?"

"Torched. Thrown in the incinerator. That's a lot of meat and you wouldn't want to attract any bears now, would you?"

Benji says nothing. He's thinking that if he were a judge, he'd give Buster a verdict of not guilty. See you, tough guy. Nice knowing you.

Benji's last respects are interrupted by a loud beeping noise erupting from Vicky's vest.

"You expecting a phone call?" asks Ozzie.

"It's Triple Seven."

Benji lightens up a bit. "You gave her a collar *and* a cell phone?"

"No, silly. It's a pager, not a phone." Vicky reaches into a pocket and switches it off. "I have it programmed to her collar's radio frequency. This morning I set the pager to go off if she comes anywhere within three miles of camp. I don't want her sniffing around here like Buster did."

Half an hour later, the bear crew, including Benji, is in Siku's helicopter homing in once again on Triple Seven. As usual, Ozzie glasses all around while Vicky flips through her field book. "This is perfect timing actually," she says. "We can give her a strong message to clear out of the camp area *and* collect the data we missed last time." Flip, flip. "Ozzie, what was the date of that capture at Bliss Lake?"

"July 24th, I believe," he says without lowering his binos.

Flip. "Ah, here it is. Yes, we still need to take more blood for DNA testing and get those cubs tagged, measured, and weighed before winter sets in."

"And tattooed," says Benji sitting in his usual back seat.

"That's affirmative, Benji," says Vicky. "Are you gunning for my job or something?"

Benji laughs while looking through the new pair of high-powered binoculars his father gave him. "You never know, Vicky. What kind of tattoos do you . . . wait a sec . . . there . . . Ozzie . . . by that little pond. Is that her?"

Ozzie whips his binos over to Benji's window then wolf-whistles into his headset. "Good spotting, kid. Do we give prizes for this sort of thing, Vicky? This kid's got a future in wildlife work."

"Give him Triple Seven's old satellite collar," she says, "the one she autographed with her fangs. It's ancient technology, no good to us. Where is she, Benji?"

Triple Seven's satellite collar! he thinks. Now *that* I could see on my wall . . . "Oh, right . . . she's at ten o'clock, on a patch of rock. Far side of the pond."

"Got her," says Vicky.

Benji watches the blonde bear rise stiffly and stretch her legs. The cubs cling to her haunches and look back at the helicopter with obvious fear.

"Looks like we woke her up," says Ozzie. "I'm surprised she'd let us ambush her right out in the open."

Siku eases back and waits for orders. "I guess she's not in the mood for cat-and-mouse games. Maybe out partying with Buster last night."

As she starts running, Benji notices that she puts hardly any weight on one leg, which gives her a clumpy gait. "She sure is running funny." He looks over to Ozzie. "Is that the bum roll you were telling me about?"

Ozzie, who has been loading the dart gun, picks up his binos again. "That ain't normal, Benji. . . . Wait a minute . . . there's blood all over her shoulder. Pretty messed up. Looks like her and Buster had a bit of a tiff."

"Let's get down to business, Siku," says Vicky. "I don't want to disturb her more than we have to and risk further injuries. Are you ready to fire, Ozzie?"

Benji hears Ozzie cursing under his breath as he hauls back on the rifle bolt. "Gimme a minute. The gun's jammed!"

The bear breaks into an awkward gallop. She is running down the center of a shallow creek, sending up sheets of spray like a protective shield. The cubs do their best to keep up, but she has to stop now and then as they flounder in the water or slip on the rocks.

"Hold back, Siku," orders Vicky. "Come on, Ozzie. We don't have all day."

Ozzie pulls back so hard he snaps the rifle bolt clean off. "Sorry, boss. The dart gun's buggered." He rummages through some gear at his feet. "We could use the net gun."

Vicky turns around and gives him a funny look. "How are you going to capture a whole bear family with one net?"

"Ah, good point. . . . Let's dart her in a week or so when she's feeling better."

"Fine, Ozzie. But I still want to shoo her out of the red zone."

"What's that?" asks Benji.

Ozzie passes him a map. "See that red circle around the mine?"

"Uh-huh."

"You've heard of No-Man's Land? Well this is No-*Bear's* Land. Any grizzlies wandering within five miles of camp are politely escorted off the premises."

"Just like Buster?"

"Exactly."

Siku drops the nose of the helicopter, quickly losing elevation and gaining speed. The bear's spray gets so high it sometimes hides her from view. The cubs scramble along beside her.

Benji tosses the map back to Ozzie and pulls out his video camera. The aerial sweep continues. Triple Seven gallops headlong down the creek. Wait till I show this flick in class, thinks Benji.

"Wait a minute, Vicky," says Ozzie. "This map tells me Triple Seven's headed for trouble."

"What's the matter?"

"I've never flown much back here. What happens to the creek up ahead?"

"I don't know. Flows into that lake up there, I guess. Victory Lake."

"Well, my map shows a nasty drop just before it. Looks like a slot canyon."

"The drillers call it 'Lovers' Leap'," says Siku. "Been poking around that hole for weeks trying to figure out what's going on with the rocks. Pretty weird, all right."

"What hole?" asks Vicky.

"Never seen it myself," says Siku. "They say it's carpeted with diamonds."

With the helicopter still on her tail, Triple Seven barrels straight for the canyon. An icy feeling of dread slithers into Benji's stomach. He lowers the camera to watch the rising drama with naked eyes. As if entering a dream, he feels certain he's watched this act before.

"That's enough, Siku," says Vicky. "We just passed the five-mile mark. She's out of the red zone."

Siku pulls back and sends the helicopter into a tight, ascending turn. The bear keeps running. She doesn't look back. She plows on through the water sending huge angel-wings of spray into the air all around her.

As the helicopter turns, Benji twists around in his seat, desperately trying to keep Triple Seven in view. In the creeping dread of this moment, he feels like he is running frantically beside her through the boulders.

Siku levels off and hovers. "I don't like it," he says with an unusual edge to his voice.

Vicky looks up from her field book. "Oh my God! She can't see where she's going with all that spray. She'll go over the edge!"

"You gotta save her!" yells Benji, not recognizing the panic in his voice.

Without waiting for orders, Siku cranks the throttle to full power and zooms the helicopter into a wide arc around the creek.

"What are you doing, Siku?" shouts Vicky.

"Sorry for jumping the gun, boss, but I think we oughta head her off at the pass. Meet her head on in the opposite direction."

"What? And scare her back into camp?" asks Benji

"Just a quick nudge, Benji," says Ozzie, "Get her to slam on the brakes before she runs blind into that hole. Go for it, Siku!"

But they arrive too late. By the time they reach the spot where the creek drops out of sight down a black crevice, the mother bear is gone. Her cubs cling to each other along the edge, looking up at the helicopter, then down into the crevice. Terror above, terror below.

"Maybe she's hiding," suggests Benji weakly. "She's good at that, isn't she?"

No one answers. Everyone's looking for a lost lame bear.

Siku circles over the crevice, then follows it to where the creek flows out of a slot canyon into Victory Lake. Looking upstream, into a narrow crack in the ancient bedrock, they see only shadows.

Benji tries to zoom in on the canyon but his video camera goes all blurry. It can't focus on the darkness. "If Triple Seven fell down there, she's gotta be a goner," he says, mostly to himself.

Again no one answers him.

Then it hits him. Like someone punched him in the stomach. Benji's so busted up inside, he feels like he fell down that hole with the bear. Something cracks and a locked-away memory rushes out through the splinters.

It happened last year. He is leaning out his attic window, waving good-bye to his mother. She is off to the library with a load of books in her arms. She smiles up at him, waits for a green light, then steps onto the street. A speeding car swerves into the crosswalk. She screams. Benji screams. Tires screech. Books fly. She flies. Benji flings out his arms as if to catch her—as she'd caught him years ago when he almost fell out this window.

She lands face down on the pavement. Benji can't watch. He spins around, looking up into the face of a crouching gargoyle, the she-bear with stone claws. . . .

Benji covers his face and sobs in the back of the helicopter.

CHAPTER 20

BEAR HUGGERS

The rule about bears is their unpredictability.
—Anonymous

"If we hurry, we'll catch the next plane to the zoo."

"Stow it, Siku!" Vicky snaps. She's in no mood for his dry humor. Slung below the helicopter in a fine mesh net is a bundle of bears—two tranquilized grizzly cubs bound for Saber Diamond Mine. Benji glumly watches them as they swing in and out of view.

Having given their mother up for dead, the biologists had no choice but to capture the cubs and haul them back to camp. The plan is to ship them out on the Hercules to the Winnipeg zoo.

They found the cubs huddled together above the hole where their mother disappeared. Ozzie bagged them with one clean shot from his net gun.

Siku brings the helicopter to a standstill high over the camp runway. Workers loading the Hercules look up at the dangling cubs. "Where do you want me to dump them?"

"Beside the trap."

Moments later, two semiconscious cubs lie sprawled inside a metal road culvert parked beside the runway. It sits on a wheeled carriage and is sealed at both ends with heavy guillotine doors. Above a tiny barred window are the words *WARNING! BEAR TRAP. DO NOT INSERT FINGERS. YOU MAY NOT GET THEM BACK.*

Another bear show begins. Though it's not yet coffee break, workers stream out of nowhere, anxious to see the captive cubs.

"Aren't they adorable!" says one of the loading crew.

"Real cute!" says an oversized driller whose overalls are black with grime.

"I wish my kid were here," says the air traffic controller who ran out of the flight shack with his headset still on.

"Where can I rent one of these?" asks a haul truck driver covered in dust.

Even the Irish cook, with her hands caked in pastry dough, runs over to stick her nose in the trap window. "Oh my, what little darlin's!"

A spontaneous lineup forms behind the window. "One at a time," says Vicky, sounding like a zookeeper. "We don't want to spook them."

It's Benji's turn. He aims his camera through the bars. Captured on video are two cowering cubs still clinging to each other in a dozy, drug-induced stupor. They lie belly to belly, with forepaws draped loosely around each other's necks. "You okay?" At the sound of Benji's voice, the female cub tilts her head up and squeaks. The runt has enough spunk left to take a weak swipe near Benji's face then collapse on his sister. How pathetic, he thinks.

Even Siku takes a turn. "Don't stick your nose in too far, or they might rip it off," he says over Benji's shoulder.

Siku peers through the bars then shakes his head. "Poor suckers. They'll be as good as dead in a zoo."

"A zoo's the only answer," says Vicky. "They wouldn't last a day out here alone. It's a nice place. I used to work there. They'll feed him good."

"Sure. Lots of goodies. But it'll kill their spirit. Look at them. They're already dead inside." Siku pushes his nose dangerously close to the window. "My grandfather says they know what we're thinking. Imagine having to listen to all the hogwash leaking from a thousand staring humans every day for the rest of your life."

Benji shakes his head and stares blankly out at the cubs' tundra home.

"There's no choice, Benji," says Vicky in an almost motherly tone. "I don't like it much either."

"Whadya mean? You said you worked there."

Vicky peers at the cubs. "Yeah . . . I used to clean the bear cages." She sighs. "I'd sweep bear dung and popcorn off the cement floors. There was this female grizzly . . . Queenie. She'd sit in her cage just rocking back and forth for *hours*. When they let her into an outside compound, she'd spend all day pacing from one side of the bars to the other, always stepping in exactly the same spots. She wore paw prints so deep into the ground they finally had to cement that over, too." Vicky abruptly looks up at Benji. "Would you mind filming the cubs? I forgot my camera."

"Sure."

Benji films the whole bear show: people streaming in to admire the cubs, Vicky hastily dispersing the crowd, her and Ozzie pushing the bear trap up the Hercules ramp, and the closing of the rear cargo door which seals two tundra grizzlies inside the belly of the monster plane. Benji swings around to get a closeup shot of Vicky's face. She is slowly shaking her head and whispering something. When she realizes Benji is filming her, she covers her eyes and walks away with her head down, still shaking. Benji lowers his camera, suddenly feeling like a peeping Tom.

Today there is an unusual crowd at the biologists' lunch table. After Buster's raid last night, the shooting, and this morning's capture of two orphaned cubs, it seems everyone wants to talk about bears.

"Where did you scoop the cubs?" a driller asks Vicky as he tears a knife through a thick steak.

"Beside Victory Lake, by that hole you guys call 'Lovers' Leap.'"

"Where's their mom?" asks the cook.

"Down the hole," says Siku bluntly.

The cook gasps and accidentally covers her mouth with pastry flour.

Vicky turns back to the driller. She's on to something, thinks Benji. "Siku tells me your crew did some drilling down there. Find anything?"

The driller shrugs. "Not yet. But I've never seen a rock formation like that up here. Slot canyon, I mean. Probably a diamond pipe down there."

"Or a good seam of gold," says another driller from way down the table. "All we've found so far is water."

"Water?" say Vicky and Ozzie together, turning to the second driller.

"Yeah," he says. "The rock's very soft down there. Water everywhere. Dark and narrow, too. Almost impossible to drag a drill in."

"Have you tried?" asks Vicky, almost leaning into her soup.

"Not yet. But I walked in once. Almost drowned," he says, laughing. "The creek's carved out a nice little swimming pool below that hole. I threw a leaded rope in there and never hit bottom."

Vicky gives Ozzie a penetrating stare. "Do you know what this means?"

Ozzie twiddles his beard. Siku twiddles his toothpick. Suddenly, Ozzie smacks his hands together and laughs. Siku grins and starts tapping his toothpick on the table faster and faster.

Benji's heart leaps. "You mean . . ."

Ozzie slaps him on the back. "Cross your fingers. Triple Seven takes to water like a duck. I've watched her plow headfirst into a lake like an Olympic diver. If any bear could survive Lovers' Leap, she could."

Inside Benji, the morning's cloud lifts. "So the cubs aren't orphans." Then he adds excitedly, "You won't have to ship them out?"

Vicky looks up. "Good point. Siku, get that net back on your chopper."

"Time for a family reunion?" he asks.

"Correct. . . . No, wait. We don't have much time. Forget the net. We'll toss the cubs right in the back."

"Like last time?" Benji asks eagerly.

"Like last time," she says in a warm way that Benji's never seen before. "Right on your lap." Vicky raises a finger to Ozzie and is about to give him some orders when everyone hears the low rumble of Hercules engines starting up. All heads swing toward the runway.

Benji hardly breathes.

"No!" cries Vicky. "They can't go!"

"Call the flight shack," says Ozzie. "We gotta stop that plane!" But nobody's got a cell phone, not even Vicky.

Ozzie jumps to his feet, knocking the driller's steak into his lap. "Sorry, pal. I've got a plane to catch." He sprints for the door leading to the runway. As the door flings open, the Hercules' rumble turns to a roar.

Benji rushes out in time to see Ozzie dash into the middle of the runway even as the Hercules starts taxiing straight for him. Ozzie frantically waves his arms at the huge aircraft and jumps up and down like a jack-in-the-box. But the pilot can't see him over the plane's big black nose. The Herc accelerates, making such a racket that Ozzie has to plug his ears while jumping around in front of it.

Still the Herc advances like a giant dragon moving into high gear. Ozzie waits as long as he dares, then leaps out of its path and runs for the flight shack. A mountain of gray dust rises behind the plane as its four giant motors strain for full power.

Instead of marveling at the plane, Benji is wondering if he could stand visiting the cubs in a zoo.

"Benji, come on!" says Vicky, running to the environmental lab. "I need your help."

"What?"

"Come on!"

Benji sprints after her, and they duck inside out of the noise.

"I need to get a GPS hit on Triple Seven," says Vicky. The lab windows shake with the Herc's thunder while she hauls out her telemetry box and flicks to her favorite bear's frequency. "Okay. I'm getting some numbers. Fire them to me while I check the wall map."

Benji reads her the locator coordinates flashing on the screen.

Vicky carefully tracks her finger along the map until it stops dead on Lovers' Leap. "She *is* still down there! Swimming about . . . I hope."

"What about life signs?" asks Benji. "Heartbeat or something."

"I wish. That transmitter in her collar suddenly died two days ago."

"Buster chewed it?"

"Could be . . ."

Benji and Vicky turn to each other at the same moment. The windows stop rattling. The roar drops to a rumble. They look out to see the Herc grinding to a halt near the end of the runway.

"Way to go, Ozzie!" says Benji.

As Vicky snaps the telemetry box shut, Benji has a disturbing thought. "So what'll Triple Seven do if the cubs are all smothered in human stink?"

"Good point. Hopefully she'll ignore it. Or else . . ."

"Or else what?"

"She'll abandon them . . . or kill them on the spot."

As Vicky hoped, the cubs are still woozy enough to carry, lap style, in the back of the helicopter, one for Ozzie, one for Benji.

"This is what I call close encounters with a grizzly bear," declares Benji as he strokes the runt male panting softly on his knees.

"What do you think it means, Ozzie?" asks Vicky. "If it was such a soft landing, why is Triple Seven still in there?"

"After a year of breathing down her back you'd think we'd be able to figure her out. But, as usual, I can't."

Benji taps Siku on the shoulder. "Your grandfather told you that bears can read our minds. Does it ever work both ways—I mean, people reading theirs?"

Siku doesn't answer for a long time. "Well, kid," he finally says, "that's not something any science project will tell you. We could study bears like this for a thousand years and they'll always keep us guessing."

"Would your grandfather know what Triple Seven's up to?" asks Benji.

"My grandfather would leave her alone."

Benji notices Vicky fiddling with her telemetry box. "Getting any beeps?"

"Locater beacon loud and clear."

Siku is soon circling over the black hole that swallowed Triple Seven. Benji sees only darkness. But, strangely, in that murky pit he also sees hope.

"Maybe that driller hallucinated the swimming pool," suggests Siku. "Mighta had water on the brain or something."

"We'll know soon enough," says Ozzie.

"What's the plan, boss?" asks Siku.

"We'll land by Victory Lake, right where the creek leaves the canyon, dump the cubs, then fade back while they wake up. My hope is that as soon as they see us, they'll deke into the canyon and run into their mother's arms."

"What if she's badly injured or rejects them?" asks Ozzie.

"We'll cross that bridge when we come to it."

The cubs behave exactly as Vicky predicted. The tranquilizer wears off soon after they land. The cubs lick each other's faces, then wander over to the creek for a long drink.

"The drugs make them thirsty," explains Ozzie as Benji captures the scene on film. Perhaps startled by Ozzie's voice, both cubs look up at the parked helicopter, then bolt for the shelter of the canyon.

Benji films their little bums disappearing into the shadows. He films the gurgling creek flowing beside the helicopter's orange floats. Later he even films Vicky making notes in her field book, Siku grinding a toothpick to pulp, and Ozzie snoring in the seat beside him. After an hour crammed into a stuffy, grounded helicopter with no bears to watch and nothing to film, Benji's restless. "Now what?"

Vicky turns to him. "Like I said, we wait. Be patient."

Ozzie chuckles. "New word in your vocabulary, Vic?"

"Shh."

Later Benji asks, "Why can't we go in and see what they're doing?"

"With their mom in the mood I think she's in," says Ozzie, "you'd be wearing a bearskin suit inside out pretty quick."

Benji eyes a carpet of cranberries beside the creek. "How about some berry-picking?"

"I want to be ready to power up instantly," says Vicky, "in case the cubs try to escape. Just sit—"

Siku cuts her off with a raised hand. "Listen!"

"What's up, skipper?" says Ozzie.

"Somebody's coming."

Ozzie opens his door and hangs out the side with his ear cocked to the canyon.

"Whadya see?" asks Benji.

"Nothing," says Siku.

"Whadya hear?"

"Nothing."

Benji laughs. "Not *this* again." He grabs his camera and zooms in on the canyon mouth. His lens struggles to focus on the darkness. Everything's fuzzy. The camera jiggles to the pounding of his heart. Then . . . something big and blonde moves slowly out of the shadows. "It's her," he says in a hushed voice. His camera clears. Filling the frame is Triple Seven, standing tall and defiant in the middle of the creek. Her mouth opens wide, followed a split second later by a bellowing roar.

Benji slowly lowers the camera, his grin as big as Triple Seven's roar is loud, and leans back into his seat.

"Does anyone see the cubs?" asks Vicky after a moment of total silence.

"Negative, boss," says Ozzie looking through his binos. "She's lookin' good though. Besides that shoulder gash Buster gave her, I see no new injuries. That bear deserves a gold medal in high diving."

Benji feels a knot untie in his belly . . . at least until Siku breaks in.

"Do you think she ate them?" he asks.

"Her paws and muzzle are clean," says Ozzie. "No fresh blood. If she ate her cubs, she did an awfully neat job."

Benji ditches his camera and picks up his new binoculars. He spots two shapes just breaking the surface of a little pool beside Triple Seven. "There's your answer."

Ozzie spots them next. "Well, I'll be. . . . They're snorkeling right beside her."

Vicky hops out of the helicopter for a better look. "Good spotting, Benji. . . . What are you doing next summer?"

The cubs emerge from the water only after the helicopter is high overhead. Triple Seven stands there looking up at it, barely moving a muscle. "She almost looks stuffed!" says Benji as he films his last view of the mighty monarch far below.

"Kid, she came mighty close to that," says Siku, lifting them above the dark canyon.

They fly over the black hole that swallowed Triple Seven and the boulder creek down which she blindly ran. The morning's journey passes beneath them like a rewinding videotape. Benji closes his eyes. The tape runs on. He sees a bear sleeping, charging, fleeing, swimming. He sees a bear standing tall with raised claws. He sees a cub playing with a moth, lying on his lap, hanging limp in Buster's jaws. These images swirl around the face of Triple Seven, whose eyes glow with a fierce, green fire.

Benji opens his eyes to the sprawling tundra below, adorned with a quilt of fall colors he's never noticed before. Its vastness once made his skin crawl. Now it makes him want to shout. Instead of a gutless speck, Benji feels like a wave on a living sea that stretches beyond the arctic to his California home. Riding this same sea, moved by the same winds, is a she-bear called Triple Seven.

In the back of the helicopter where he once wept, Benji is flooded with a new warmth that goes beyond the rebirth of Triple Seven and the reunion with her cubs. A missing piece in the puzzle of his life slips into place—his mother, like Triple Seven, there in his heart forever.

Back in the environmental lab, Ozzie goes straight for his locker and digs out Triple Seven's old, chewed-up satellite collar. He walks over to Benji, who is studying bear movements drawn on Vicky's wall map. "Here, Benji. You earned it."

Benji turns around and his jaw drops. "Awesome!"

Ozzie whistles sharply to get Vicky and Siku's attention, then ceremoniously puts the collar over Benji's head. Speaking with an Old English accent, he holds his arms up and says, "Sir Benjamin Gloss, for showing valor in the face of tooth and claw, for having the eyes of an eagle, and for sowing hope and faith among doubters like us, I hereby dub thee Right Honorable Bear Hugger Extraordinaire."

Siku starts clapping. Vicky joins in, and soon they are all comparing notes on the day's adventure. Ozzie pulls a fresh bag of marshmallows out of his locker and passes them around with great pomp and circumstance. As he offers a handful to Benji he gives him a quizzical look. "Hey. Where's your diamond? Somebody steal it in your sleep?"

Benji laughs and rubs the spot on his eyebrow where it used to be. "No . . . I . . . ah . . . yanked it out. I found it bugged me when I was bear watching through binoculars."

"Oh, I see," says Ozzie smiling.

The party mood is broken by a loud knock at the door.

"Who in the world?" says Vicky. "Nobody ever knocks for . . ."

In walks Benji's father, brushing the runway dust off his suit jacket.

"Well, I'll be," says Ozzie.

"Dad! When did you get here?"

"So *here* you are," says Gloss. "Flew in this morning."

"To what do we owe this honor, sir?" asks Ozzie, offering him a marshmallow.

Gloss raises an open palm. "No, thanks. I'm trying to quit. Heh-heh." He pulls Benji's new binoculars out of a bag. "The mechanic found these in the helicopter. Saw the name *Gloss* on them and naturally figured they were mine. I thought you might need them if you go on any more bear hunts."

Benji is about to reach for them when he remembers the chewed bear collar around his neck. His father looks at it with raised eyebrows. "So what's all *this* about?"

"It's a long story, Dad. I'll tell you later if you have time." He takes the binoculars and blows dust off the lenses. "Thanks again for the binos. They helped us find Triple Seven."

"Who?"

Benji looks over at Vicky who has an uncommon smile on her face. "One of your collared bears, Dad. Don't worry. *She* won't give you any trouble."

Gloss stands with his hands on his hips, looking at Benji. "One of the bear people now, eh?"

"Just keepin' an eye on these guys for you, Dad. So they don't blow all your money."

Gloss smiles. "Your mother would be proud." He nods to the collar. "So how do these babies work anyway? They sure cost enough," he says, darting a mock threatening glance at Vicky.

"Here, Dad. Try it on."

Benji is about to put Triple Seven's collar around his father's neck when somebody's cell phone goes off.

Benji laughs out loud when he sees his father, Vicky, and Ozzie thump their chests at the same time, trying to find their phones. Siku shakes his head and covers his grinning face.

It's his father's. "Ralph here," he says, walking toward the door. "Yep . . . okay . . . right away." He waves to Benji on the way out. "Gotta go, son. Meetings. Might see you at supper."

"Sure, Dad."

As the door slams, Ozzie slaps Benji on the back. "I guess some of us already wear electronic leashes," he says, waving his cell phone around. "Who needs a bear collar when you've got one of these?"

"A blessing and a curse, eh, Vicky?" says Siku.

Vicky fixes her eyes on Siku for a moment. "Which reminds me," she says playfully. "Benji, I'd like to give you one more honor." Vicky untangles a silver chain around her neck. "Ah, here it is," she says, holding a shiny red key.

Siku spits out his toothpick.

A half-eaten marshmallow slips from Ozzie's fingers. He shoots Vicky a puzzled look. "You're not *serious.*"

"Uh-huh."

"But you've still got almost two year's worth of data to collect on Triple Seven. You'll be throwing it all away if you pop her collar now."

"So sue me," she says with that smile again. "We've learned all anyone ever could about that bear. The collar gave us a magic window on Triple Seven's world. But I think she's telling us loud and clear that it's time to draw the curtains. I'm sure Benji's father would agree that we got our money's worth out of her."

Vicky hands the key to Benji. "Here you go, Sir Benjamin. May the honor of freeing Triple Seven be yours." She hefts the telemetry box onto the table, flips open the leather case adorned with wild animals, and records some final coordinates into her field book.

Benji is speechless.

"Go for it, kid," says Siku. "That bear will know who pulled the plug. It'll be good medicine for both of you."

"What about the collar?" asks Benji. "I thought you said those new ones cost over five thousand bucks."

"No problem, Benji," says Vicky. "It's not as if it'll stop transmitting the minute you pop it. That thing will keep beeping for at least another two years. We'll scoop it tomorrow. You can come with us for a final joyride. Take the front seat."

"Whatever you say, boss." Benji sticks the red detonator key into the slot and gives it a lively twist.

CHAPTER 21

VICTORY LAKE

A grizzly bear is always smarter than your average grizzly bear
   researcher.
—*Rob Wieglus, Bear Biologist*

They never do find the collar. By the time Benji flips the detonator key and pops it off, the family of bears is swimming across
Victory Lake. The mother bear chooses the fastest route away from
the mining camp—straight west across the water.

A slight electric pulse tickles her neck at the moment of det-
onation. For a split second a silvery necklace of tiny bubbles
adorns the swimming bear's neck. Then the heavy collar falls
away and sinks like a stone, almost bopping a good-sized lake
trout on the way to the bottom of the lake. From way down
there, in the cold dark muck, it faithfully transmits a steady
stream of beeps to a satellite spinning five hundred miles above
the earth.

About halfway across Victory Lake is a distinct narrows formed
by a huge esker that sticks out into the water from both sides.
Because of its handy location in the middle of a big lake and its
link to an esker highway hundreds of miles long, this sandy bot-

tleneck acts like a biological magnet for migrating caribou and the host of other animals that follow them.

Swimming freer now, without the drag of her bulky collar, the mother bear steers a course straight for the narrows. She comes ashore on a small beach along the north side. Here the esker slopes gently out of the water, up through a patch of thick moss to a tall granite boulder sticking straight out of the ground. The rock is shaped in an almost perfect rectangle, presenting a tombstone-smooth face to each of the four poles of the compass. On the rock's crown is a wide gash, carved eons ago when this lone sentinel of the tundra drew a lightning bolt from the sky.

As the three bears clamber ashore and shake walls of water on one another, an arctic hare shoots out from under the big rock to see what's going on. It sits motionless except for the occasional chew on some grass hanging out of its mouth. The hare's coat is once again almost completely white, magically etched by the looming shadow of winter. It watches the bears lick drops of water off one another's faces until the cubs catch its scent and give chase up the hill. Their mother shows no interest in the hare and woofs them back to the beach. She wants to show them something special about this place.

The mother bear noses them behind her, then starts slowly ambling straight for the rock. Padding through the fragrant red and green mosses, she picks up a pronounced trail made not by caribou, wolves, or foxes. She leads her cubs up a path worn deep into the tundra by generations of grizzlies, each walking precisely in the steps of the one that went before. The cubs do their best to stretch out their legs and plant their little paws in the huge print craters trod by their mother, and her mother, and thousands of grizzlies before them. Somehow the cubs know, even on their first visit, that this trail is theirs and theirs alone.

It's a short parade to the rock. The mother bear carefully sniffs all around its base. She reads the scent inscriptions of every grizzly that has passed this way over the last few weeks—a young male and his sister, another mother and her two yearling cubs, an old aunt of hers who she thought was dead long ago.

She rears up on her hind legs to rub her neck and shoulders against the rock's well-polished surface. With satisfied grunts and raspy sighs she digs and scratches at the chronic itch spots and matted fur that, for so long, were hidden and out of reach below her collar. As she rubs, her forepaws wave back and forth before her, totally relaxed. Soon her whole body is almost dancing with pleasure. She raises her muzzle to the sky at the exquisite sweetness of a good scratch against a much treasured bear rock.

The cubs get into the act and rock and roll beside her, trying to share in their mother's joy. She playfully knocks them both over with one kick, then settles down against the rock and makes soft cooing sounds. The cubs crawl to her and suckle.

With a triumphant sense of belonging, the mother bear leans back and quietly surveys the circle of her tundra kingdom. Then, unleashed from the probing eyes and ears of human beings, the bear family rises, stretches, and melts into the vast arctic wilderness.

ABOUT THE AUTHOR

Taking science to the streets is what Jamie Bastedo's work is all about—if you can call it work! Whether playing zany environmental songs around the campfire, hosting lively nature shows on the radio, performing as an arctic explorer, directing science videos, running outdoor education camps, leading ecotours, or writing about some marvel of nature, Jamie spreads a catching enthusiasm and love for the land. Well established as a popular science writer, he has written four books on northern nature, including *Reaching North: A Celebration of the Subarctic* and *Shield Country: The Life and Times of the Oldest Piece of the Planet.* He also has penned more than thirty natural history features in numerous magazines, including *Up Here, Backpacker,* and *Winter Living.* The idea for *Tracking Triple Seven* was born in the back of a helicopter while Jamie was working as a field biologist in the central arctic barren-lands. When not out on the land, he hangs his hat in Yellowknife, Northwest Territories, where he lives with his wife and two daughters.